How to Rescue a Family

Teri Wilson

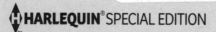

HARLEQUIN® SPECIAL EDITION

Special thanks and acknowledgment are given to Teri Wilson for her contribution to the Furever Yours series.

Recycling programs
for this product may
not exist in your area.

ISBN-13: 978-1-335-57368-1

How to Rescue a Family

Copyright © 2019 by Harlequin Books S.A.

Printed in U.S.A.

"I'm sure he's close by."

She reached for Ryan as naturally as if touching him was something she'd done a million times. A zing of electricity shot through her and she snatched her hand back. "Um..."

Their eyes met and held, but then Ryan's gaze drifted over her head. "There he is!"

Sure enough, Dillon stood behind them, less than three feet away. He was facing one of the kennels, staring intently at the dog inside—Tucker.

"Oh." Amanda blinked.

Well, this is an interesting development.

"This is Tucker. He's a little—" *aloof, cranky, irritable* "—bashful."

Dillon, however, remained glued to the spot as if he'd just spotted his new best friend.

So she relented. "But if you want to pet him, we can give it a try."

She cast a pleading glance at the dog as she unfastened the lock on the kennel door. *Be nice.*

Before she could instruct Dillon on how to pet the picky dog, Tucker closed his eyes and burrowed into his touch.

What was happening?

As Amanda carried Tucker inside, she whispered into his furry ear, "Whatever has come over you, keep it up. This little boy needs a friend."

FUREVER YOURS: Finding forever homes— and hearts!—has never been so easy.

Dear Reader,

Welcome back to Spring Forest, North Carolina, and Furever Paws Animal Rescue! I'm so thrilled to be part of the Harlequin Special Edition Furever Yours continuity. This is the first multiauthored series I've ever worked on, and I've loved every minute of it. I'm a huge animal lover, and as soon as I heard about Furever Yours, I was over the moon.

How to Rescue a Family is book two in the series, and it takes up where the first book, *A New Leash on Love*, left off. Birdie, Bunny and the animals at Furever Paws are still reeling in the aftermath of a recent tornado, but Amanda Sylvester, the manager and co-owner of the Main Street Grille, has a plan that just might help put the shelter back together.

This is a story about people struggling to form bonds with one another. Just like in real life, the unconditional love of a pet helps them deal with the pain of the past and find the happy-ever-after they deserve. Amanda, Ryan and Dillon set out to rescue Tucker, but in the end, the cranky little dog and these wonderful people end up rescuing each other.

I hope you enjoy reading *How to Rescue a Family* as much I loved writing it. Don't forget to check out the other books in the Furever Yours series to find out what else is in store for Birdie, Bunny and the sweet animals at Furever Paws!

Happy reading,

Teri Wilson

Teri Wilson is a novelist for Harlequin. She is the author of *Unleashing Mr. Darcy*, now a Hallmark Channel Original Movie. Teri is also a contributing writer at hellogiggles.com, a lifestyle and entertainment website founded by Zooey Deschanel that is now part of the *People* magazine, *Time* magazine and *Entertainment Weekly* family. Teri loves books, travel, animals and dancing every day. Visit Teri at teriwilson.net or on Twitter, @teriwilsonauthr.

Books by Teri Wilson

Harlequin Special Edition

Wilde Hearts

The Ballerina's Secret
How to Romance a Runaway Bride
The Bachelor's Baby Surprise
A Daddy by Christmas

Drake Diamonds

His Ballerina Bride
The Princess Problem
It Started with a Diamond

HQN Books

Unmasking Juliet
Unleashing Mr. Darcy

Visit the Author Profile page at Harlequin.com for more titles.

For Bliss, Finn and Princess,
the very best dogs in the world.

Chapter One

"He's here."

Amanda Sylvester looked up from the pear-and-goat-cheese puff pastry she was assembling and found Belle Ross, her head waitress, grinning at her from ear to ear.

"You know, in case you've decided to take a chance and actually speak to him." Belle lifted a brow. "Just saying."

"The lunch rush is in full swing. Shouldn't you be waiting tables?" Amanda reached for a fresh rosemary sprig from the tiny garden she'd planted in the Grille's sole kitchen window and placed it carefully on top of her creation. *Just saying.*

Belle leaned against the door frame. "It's three o'clock. The lunch crowd disappeared almost an hour ago. But nice try, boss."

"Oh." Amanda had lost track of time—*again*—a common occurrence when she was experimenting with new recipes. Not that any of her new dishes ever actually turned up on the menu.

A girl could dream, though, right?

"He ordered a latte to go. I reminded him, yet again, that we're not exactly a latte sort of establishment. We're basically a diner, so our coffee offerings are pretty much limited to regular and decaf." Belle shoved a paper cup at Amanda. "This is his coffee—regular, by the way. You're giving it to him. I refuse to do it myself."

Amanda stared at the cup. "Um."

"Seriously, take it. This secret crush of yours is getting old."

Amanda's face went hot, and she defiantly plucked the coffee from Belle's grasp. "It's *not* a secret crush. I just think he's mysterious, that's all."

Nor was he terrible to look at, but that was beside the point.

Mostly.

Amanda had lived in Spring Forest, North Carolina, her entire life. She'd worked at her family's restaurant, Main Street Grille, since she was old enough to juggle more than one plate at a time. She loved it. She really did. But sometimes, it was all just a little predictable.

Which explained her fascination with the man who'd suddenly started showing up multiple times a day, looking as if he'd just walked out of the pages of *GQ* rather than any of the redbrick buildings in Spring Forest's historic downtown district. Ryan Carter, the new owner and editor-in-chief of *The Spring Forest*

Chronicle, wasn't exactly what people might call personable, but he was certainly different. And attractive.

In a brooding sort of way.

Belle grinned. "Keep telling yourself that, boss."

"You're so fired," Amanda whispered as she slipped past her, toward the dining room.

She was kidding, obviously. Belle was a ridiculously competent waitress, as well as one of Amanda's oldest friends. But she was also delusional.

It *wasn't* a crush. Amanda was a grown woman. A *career* woman. Twenty-nine-year-old ambitious adults didn't have crushes.

But when she reached the counter and Mr. Tall-Dark-and-Grumpy glanced up from the iPhone in his hand, her stomach flipped in a way that could only be described as crush-tastic.

Get a grip on yourself. That's not even a word.

She squared her shoulders, smiled and offered him the cup. "Your coffee."

He took it. "Thank you very much."

No smile. No indication that he thought she, herself, was crush-tastic, despite the very good hair day she was having. Nothing.

He gave her a distracted nod before turning to leave.

"You're welcome," she said to his back.

Rude much?

Amanda picked up the closest dish towel and scrubbed furiously at an invisible spot on the counter. She glanced back up for another glimpse of his disappearing form as he pushed through the door and strode purposefully down Main Street. He had a lovely back. Broad and strong, as if capable of shouldering the heaviest of burdens. And were those actual muscles moving beneath the elegant weave of his suit jacket? God, they were.

"How'd it go?" Belle asked.

"Disastrously." Amanda scrubbed harder at the smooth Formica countertop. "I was confident and lovely. I smiled when I said 'Here's your coffee,' and I might have even thrown in a flirty hair flip."

"Then what happened?"

Amanda crossed her arms and sighed. "He said 'Thank you very much,' and left."

"I see what you mean. Total disaster." The corner of Belle's mouth twitched into a grin. "Clearly the man is a monster."

"You jest, but the fact that he didn't smile says something about him, don't you think?"

"Yes. It says he's in a hurry. Or distracted. Or under-caffeinated, hence the coffee." Belle gestured, Vanna White–style, at the coffeepot.

"Or he has no interest in me whatsoever, which is *fine*." More than fine, really. She didn't have time for a love interest. She didn't even have time for a dog, for crying out loud. She just wanted to do her job, post her foodie pics to Instagram and admire Ryan Carter from afar. Was that really too much to ask? "He's married, anyway. We know that much about him."

"We do?" Belle peered out the window and squinted after him, as if she expected to spot a just-married sign taped to his back.

"Of course we do. He's ordered two of the dinner

specials to go almost every day this week. There's a Mrs. Tall-Dark-and-Grumpy waiting for him at home." She paused for dramatic effect. "Obviously."

"The only thing obvious about any of this is that you're a chicken. It's like the tenth grade Sadie Hawkins dance all over again."

"Don't go there." Sure, that humiliating experience had taken place approximately fourteen years ago, but Amanda still wasn't over it. Not even close. "And I'm not a chicken. Need I remind you that I rode out a tornado all by myself last week?"

She'd been terrified out of her mind as she'd cowered in the bathroom of her tiny apartment above the Grille while the windows rattled and it sounded like a freight train was barreling through town. But she'd survived. *On her own.* The next morning, when she'd seen the storm damage, she felt kind of like Wonder Woman.

"Which reminds me." She glanced at the vintage white-gold watch on her wrist, a keepsake from her grandmother. "I need to get out to the animal shelter. I promised Birdie and Bunny I'd walk some dogs today."

Bernadette and Gwendolyn Whitaker, affectionately known throughout Spring Forest as Birdie and Bunny, were sisters who ran a local pet rescue where Amanda volunteered once a week. They lived in the same rambling Victorian the Whitaker family had called home for generations, and a number of years ago, they'd opened a small animal shelter on part of their property.

Belle winced. "How do things look out at Furever Paws? The tornado hit the shelter pretty hard, didn't it?"

"Yes, from what I hear, it touched right down on the sisters' land. They lost a lot of trees, and the shelter's roof was pretty much demolished. I'm sure their insurance will fix it, but in the meantime, it's a mess. I feel terrible about it. Birdie and Bunny are overwhelmed, and those poor animals have been through enough as it is." Amanda wished for the thousandth time that she could adopt one of the dogs.

But she was hardly ever home. It didn't seem fair, especially for a rescue dog in need of attention. In need of love.

Love.

Amanda's throat clogged. What was wrong with her? The tornado must have rattled her more than she wanted to admit.

"Well, at least you're getting out of here for a bit. Some time away from this place will do you good. You've been working since sunup."

Actually, Amanda had dragged herself into the kitchen before sunrise, but not completely out of necessity. She'd wanted to get her food prep and other responsibilities out of the way so she could have some time to experiment with the goat cheese she'd picked up at the farmer's market over the weekend.

"I want to take a few pictures of my pastry before I go." She pushed her way through the swinging door, back into the kitchen. Her sanctuary, where she'd been perfectly content until she'd been distracted once again by the brooding newspaperman.

What a colossal waste of time, as evidenced by her puff pastry, which suddenly looked significantly less puffy than it had before she'd abandoned it to deliver coffee to Mr. Cranky Pants.

"Is it supposed to look like that?" Belle said, peering over Amanda's shoulder.

"You mean sad and deflated?" Amanda slid her phone back into her pocket. She wouldn't be posting to Instagram today, after all. "No, it's not."

"It might still taste good." Ah Belle, always the optimist.

"What makes puff pastry special is its light and airy texture. I think that ship has sailed." Amanda pinned her with a glare. "Yet another reason I shouldn't be trying to flirt with a stranger over his takeout coffee order."

"Spring Forest is still a relatively small town. We could check up on him, you know. Find out more about him? Perhaps we could even be hospitable and start a conversation with Ryan himself. Then he wouldn't be a stranger anymore."

"Yes, but my pastry would still be flat." Amanda picked it up and dumped it unceremoniously into the nearest trash can.

"Maybe your social life wouldn't, though," Belle muttered.

Amanda pretended not to hear her.

She didn't need a man. She needed a good night's sleep. She needed a family member to step up and help out at the Grille. She needed enough Instagram followers to convince her mother she could successfully expand the restaurant into catering weddings and maybe even fancy galas in nearby Raleigh.

And right now, she needed to get to the animal shelter. Because dogs were much simpler than actual human relationships.

Dogs were loyal. They were honest, and they didn't grow bored, change their feelings on a whim or run away when times got tough. They were possibly the best living example of unconditional love.

Sometimes Amanda wondered how they could be so gentle and sweet, because in her experience, human beings could be quite the opposite.

Ryan Carter clutched his cardboard coffee cup and pushed through the door of *The Spring Forest Chronicle*, reminding himself once again to slow down. Breathe. Take a look around.

He wasn't in DC anymore. Things moved at a much slower pace in Spring Forest. That's why he'd moved here in the first place. After the sudden and drastic upheaval in his personal life, he'd needed a fresh start. He'd needed a soft place to land, for both himself and his son.

It had taken a little over a year of searching, but he'd found it. Spring Forest was everything they needed, an oasis dripping with Southern charm. Moving here felt like falling into a soft feather bed after a long, restless season of too little sleep.

Too little joy.

He no longer needed to drop everything he was doing in order to attend a White House press briefing without notice, and the back-to-back deadlines that so often woke him up in a cold sweat were now in his past, like so much else. He didn't even have an editor-in-chief breathing down his neck anymore. That job belonged to Ryan now.

Except *The Spring Forest Chronicle* wasn't *The Washington Post*. Not even close.

"Hello, Mr. Carter." Jonah Miller, Ryan's assistant, stood and beamed at him.

"Jonah, we talked about this. Remember? You don't need to stand every time I enter the building." He forced a smile and aimed for an expression that somewhat resembled patience. "And I want you to call me Ryan."

"Right. Sorry." Jonah's gaze dropped to Ryan's coat and tie. "I keep forgetting."

Ryan was going to have to stop wearing suits to the office. *The Spring Forest Chronicle* wasn't exactly a formal working environment, as evidenced by the Converse sneakers on Jonah's feet and the skinny jeans on the younger man's legs. Old habits died hard, though, and Ryan's closet was filled with gray flannel and pinstripes. Relics from his former life.

He made a mental note to buy some casual clothes as soon as possible. As it was, he felt more like Jonah's dad than his boss. Impossible, considering Ryan was only thirty-three and Jonah was somewhere in his early twenties. But being around all that youthful optimism made Ryan feel ancient, and the last thing he needed at the office was a reminder of his shortcomings as a father.

"Do you have any messages for me?" He shot Jonah a hopeful glance.

As much as Ryan hated to admit it, leaving his position as the political editor at the *Post* to buy a small-town newspaper was more of an adjustment than he'd expected. He missed his old job—the adrenaline rush that came with chasing a breaking story, the sense of accomplishment, the prestige. Dillon was more important than any of those things, obviously. That's why they were here.

But Ryan would have given his left arm for a story to cover—a *real* story with some meat on its bones. A story that didn't involve a bake sale or the removal of a stop sign or new uniforms for the high school marching band. The only thing truly newsworthy he'd covered recently had been the tornado that swept through town.

He could have done without that particular news item. The twister had scared Dillon so badly that he'd slept in the bathtub for three straight nights afterward. Ryan had stretched out on the bathroom floor in his sleeping bag alongside the tub, unwilling to leave his frightened son alone. His lower back was a mess.

But at least he'd been there.

For once.

"Yes, actually." Jonah tore a sheet from the pink message pad on his desk. Ryan hadn't seen a message pad like that in years. He wondered if it was left over from the building's banking days. "Patty Matthews from the elementary school called."

Ryan's jaw clenched as he stared down at the message. Mrs. Matthews was Dillon's teacher, which meant the call had zero to do with business. Worse, it might mean that there was a problem with his son.

Jonah cleared his throat. "She said she tried to reach you on your cell, but it rolled straight to voice mail."

"That's because I was at the mobile store buying a new phone. It's only been activated for a few minutes." Ryan had been so consumed with taking care of Dillon during the storm that he'd accidentally left his cell phone plugged into its charger during the tornado. Big mistake. It had been randomly powering itself down ever since, and he couldn't afford to miss any more news tips…

Or calls from his son's teacher.

"Right." Jonah nodded. "I'm sure everything's fine, but you should probably call her back."

"Of course." Dread settled in the pit of Ryan's stomach like a lead weight. Things hadn't been fine for a long, long time.

He checked his watch.

"School gets out shortly. I think I'll head over there instead of calling." He glanced at Jonah. "Unless there's something urgent I need to attend to?"

"Nope." Jonah shrugged. "There's not."

Of course there wasn't. The paper didn't even go to press for three more days. *The Spring Forest Chronicle* was a weekly publication, which gave Ryan a flexible schedule. He dropped off Dillon for school every morning, and picked him up, as well. He attended the school's aftercare program in the afternoons when Ryan was working. Before the accident, when they'd lived in DC, Ryan had never set foot inside a single one of Dillon's classrooms.

His gut churned, and the message crumpled in his fist.

What if it was too late? What if he never managed

to connect with his son? What if Dillon's retreat into silence was permanent?

It's not too late. It can't be.

"Right. I'll see you tomorrow, then." Ryan scanned the room, in case anyone else on his minuscule staff looked as though they needed to speak to him. But the other three full-time employees were all bent over their desks, eyes glued to their laptops. Ryan thought he spied a computer game on at least one of the screens.

He sighed and stalked out of the building, back onto Main. Dappled sunlight drifted through the branches of the trees lining the street, warming his face as he made his way to the large public parking lot adjacent to the Granary, where he'd left his car—a small SUV. New, like nearly everything else in his life.

Sometimes he forgot what color it was or where exactly he'd parked it. Hell, sometimes he forgot he drove that to work now instead of taking the Metro.

He just needed a little time, that's all. They both did. Eventually, this new life would feel right. It would fit, like a favorite sweater. Time heals all wounds. Isn't that what people always said?

God, he hoped so.

But he was starting to wonder. So were Maggie's parents, and that was a problem. A big one.

Ryan tipped his head back to down the rest of his coffee. He didn't want to think about his overbearing in-laws right now. Thankfully, he didn't have to. The move to Spring Forest had put nearly three hundred blissful miles between him and his late wife's mom and dad.

I'll drink to that.

He swallowed the dregs from his paper cup and turned to throw it in a nearby recycling bin, but as he did so he crashed into something. Or more accurately, some*one*. A woman.

Ooof.

She stumbled backward, and Ryan reached for her shoulders to keep her from falling. "Oh God, I'm sorry. I'm in a hurry and wasn't looking where I was going. Are you hurt?"

"Ouch," she wailed. His elbow had rammed right into her nose.

The woman's hands were covering her face, and something about her graceful fingers seemed vaguely familiar, but Ryan couldn't imagine why. He stared at her buffed nails and the slim gold bands on her middle finger and thumb, trying to figure out where he'd seen those feminine details before.

"I'm sorry." He swallowed, forcing himself to release his hold on her since she was standing perfectly still now.

His throat went thick, and he was suddenly extremely conscious of the fact that he hadn't touched a woman in quite a long time. She smelled like something decadent and sweet—vanilla, maybe. And her sweater had been soft beneath his fingertips. So soft that an ache formed deep in his chest. He inhaled a ragged breath and nearly choked.

"I'm fine, but you plowed into me pretty hard. It's okay. It's…" she peeked up at him from between her hands "…*you*."

Ryan frowned. "Me?"

"Yes." She nodded. "You."

Had they met before? Ryan would have remembered her. He was sure of it. She had a lovely bronze complexion, full lips and eyes the color of fine Southern bourbon.

But he'd been walking around in a fog for months now—looking without seeing. Existing without living.

"The diner," he said as realization dawned. "You handed me my coffee before."

Her lips curved into the smallest of smiles, and she nodded.

"It was very good, by the way." What was he doing? *Flirting?*

No.

Definitely not.

Her eyes narrowed. Somewhere in their depths, Ryan spotted flecks of gold. "See, now you're frowning again, so I don't believe you."

"I never lie about coffee," he said solemnly.

She smiled again, and it sent a zing through his chest, quickly followed by a pang of guilt.

He had no business taking delight in making this beautiful woman smile. No business whatsoever. His life was a disaster, his wife was dead, and in the year since her accident, his son hadn't uttered a word.

What would she think if she knew the ugly truth?

He didn't want to know. "I've got to go."

It came out sharper than he intended, and she flinched. But Ryan barely noticed, because he'd already begun to walk away.

Chapter Two

"Mr. Carter, I'm glad you stopped by. My teaching assistant is helping the kids pack up for the day, so we can chat for a few minutes until the bell rings." Patty Matthews, Dillon's teacher, shut the door of her classroom behind her and smiled up at Ryan as she stepped into the hallway.

Over her shoulder, he could see inside the room through the door's long, slender window. The space was an explosion of color, from the brightly hued mats covering the floor to the cheery alphabet signs on the wall—*A is for aardvark, B is for baboon, C is for camel* and so on. The cartoon animals reminded Ryan of all the times he'd promised to take Dillon to the Smithsonian Zoo when they'd lived in Washington, DC.

Promises he'd broken.

He swallowed and forced his gaze back to his son's teacher. "I got your message. Is something wrong?"

The teacher's smile dimmed. "I wouldn't necessarily say anything is wrong. Dillon is a sweet boy—very well behaved—and his mathematics level is advanced for his age, so I'm not at all concerned with his progress in that regard."

Ryan nodded, sensing the *but* that was sure to come.

"But…" *And there it was.* "This afternoon in reading circle, he refused to read aloud when it was his turn. Did Dillon experience trouble reading at his previous school?"

Ryan's gaze flitted to the classroom window again, where he could see Dillon sitting quietly as his desk, holding his favorite plastic dinosaur toy, while the students around him chatted and wiggled their backpacks onto their shoulders.

"As I explained when I met with the principal and registered Dillon for school, he's had a difficult time since his mother's death last year. He's quiet." Ryan cleared his throat. "*Very* quiet."

"Yes, Principal Martin passed that information along to me. But I'm not sure we realized the extent of Dillon's shyness. Exactly how quiet are we talking about?" Mrs. Matthews tilted her head and waited for Ryan to explain.

He probably should have made things clearer when Dillon started school at Spring Forest Elementary. Scratch that—he definitely should have done so. But he'd stopped short of telling the whole truth because he hadn't wanted his boy to start off in a brand-new school with a label hanging over his head.

It had been the wrong call, obviously. Ryan should have seen this awkward conversation coming. He was a journalist, for God's sake. Anticipating conflicts was part of what made him good at his job.

"Dillon won't read aloud," he finally said.

"Mr. Carter." Mrs. Matthews lifted a brow. "Does Dillon speak at all?"

A heaviness came over Ryan all of a sudden, as if the simple act of standing required more energy than he could muster. "No, he doesn't."

The problem wasn't physical. According to his pediatrician back in DC, it was just a temporary manifestation of grief. It wasn't permanent.

It *couldn't be* permanent.

"I see." The teacher's voice grew soft. Soothing. "It's important for me to know exactly what's going on so I can figure out how to best help your son."

"Right. I'm sorry. I'd just hoped…" He'd hoped once Dillon was in a new place, with new people, he'd be ready to open up and start over. He'd hoped leaving behind the only home his son had ever known and bringing him to Spring Forest had been the right call. Most of all, he'd hoped that it wasn't too late to be the kind of father Dillon needed.

The kind he *deserved*.

"I guess I thought he'd be happy here." Even just a little bit.

"We'll do our best to make sure he is," she said, sounding far more certain than Ryan felt.

He scrubbed a hand over his face and glanced at the window one last time, only instead of catching another glimpse of the inside of the classroom, his gaze snagged on his own reflection in the polished glass. There were lines around his eyes that hadn't been there a year ago. He looked every bit as tired as he felt.

He also looked like a pompous jerk standing in the school hallway dressed in his overly formal bespoke suit and Hermès tie—a pompous jerk who had no idea how to help his own kid.

"I took him to see a therapist a few times before we moved here, and she said the most important thing we can give Dillon is patience. At home, I've removed all pressure for him to speak. As soon as he says a word, even if it's just a whisper, I'm to offer him gentle encouragement. Other than that, I'm just supposed to let him know that I'm here and I'm not going anywhere. That's the only concrete advice she could give me."

Mrs. Matthews gave him a curt nod. "Then that's what we'll do here at school as well. From now on, I won't call on him to read aloud. During reading circle, I can send him to the library where he can read quietly on his own so he won't feel pressured in any way. And if I notice him whispering or speaking in class, I'll be sure and reward him—nothing too over the top, so he won't be singled out from the other kids. Maybe a sticker or a baseball card? Does this plan work for you?"

Ryan nodded. "It does. Thank you for your help. It means a lot."

Dillon's school in DC hadn't been so accommodating. Ryan had considered homeschooling, but there was no way he could juggle that with his workload at the *Post*. Their only option had been a completely new start.

New town, new school, new life.

"Of course. If you wait here, I'll tell him you've come to take him home. The bell will be ringing in just a few minutes." The teacher turned toward the door, then paused with her hand on the knob. "And Mr. Carter, try not to worry. We all want what's best for Dillon. He's a lucky little boy to have a father like you."

Ryan nodded his thanks as a dullness spread throughout his chest, blossoming into a familiar regret.

He's a lucky little boy to have a father like you.

If only that were true.

As soon as Amanda turned her red 1967 Chevy pickup onto Little Creek Road, dread tangled into a hard knot in the pit of her stomach. A third of the large oak trees along the old country road were down and the ones left standing had been stripped bare of their leaves. It looked like something straight out of a horror movie had come along and taken a machete to the forest, severing the top right off every white oak in sight.

Something horrific had come to their town, of course. The tornado that ravaged Spring Forest had touched down exactly a week ago.

Amanda had called to check on Bunny and Birdie the morning after the storm, so she really shouldn't have been surprised by the extent of the damage. But hearing about it and seeing it were two entirely different things.

Her hands shook on the steering wheel as the memories of that awful night came back to her—the deafening roar as the twister spun down Main Street, the horrible way her apartment windows had rattled in their frames, the cool press of the bathtub's porcelain against her cheek as she curled into a ball and did her best to ride out the storm. It was terrifying, and all in all, Spring Forest's modest downtown area had fared pretty well. She couldn't imagine how scared the Whitaker sisters must have been, not to mention the poor helpless animals in the shelter.

Her eyes filled with tears just thinking about it.

Get a grip. You're fine. Everyone *is* fine.

Still, she'd feel better as soon as she got a glimpse of Tucker, her favorite dog at Furever Paws, and made sure he wasn't traumatized. Not that she'd be able to tell, exactly. The little Chihuahua/dachshund mix—or chiweenie, as Birdie and Bunny liked to say—was notoriously standoffish. Amanda's nickname for him was Grumpy. Which, now that she thought about it, would also be a suitable moniker for Ryan Carter.

Was it weird that she seemed to be attracted to cranky men and equally cranky dogs?

Probably. But at least she was consistent.

Consistently ridiculous. She maneuvered the truck into the shelter's gravel parking lot, and rolled her eyes. So what if her tastes were a bit…odd? As she'd told Belle again and again, she didn't have time for either a pet or a boyfriend, so it really didn't matter how cranky the mysterious Mr. Carter could be. The grumpier, the better. If he looked right through her when she handed him his coffee, he'd be easier to ignore.

Except he hadn't looked right through her on the street earlier. On the contrary, he'd focused on her with such blinding intensity it had made her head spin a little. For a minute, she'd thought he might be flirting with her. He'd even been charming, in a serious, formal sort of way.

I never lie about coffee.

Was she supposed to laugh at that? She had no idea. She only knew that all the butterflies in North Carolina had seemed to gather in her tummy at once, making her feel all fluttery and wonderful.

And then his hint of a smile had flattened into a straight line and he'd left before she could process what was happening. Perfect. Just perfect.

She climbed out of the truck and slammed the door a little harder than necessary. Why was she even thinking about Ryan Carter when Furever Paws was right in front of her looking seriously worse for wear?

The fence surrounding the property was flat on the ground, and the roof of the main shelter building looked as if the entire right side had been pried off with a can opener. The damage definitely looked worse than Birdie and Bunny had let on. Much, much worse. Even with good insurance, how long would it take before everything was fully restored?

As she stood surveying the destruction, she caught a glimpse of a gray flash out of the corner of her eye. She whipped her head around, but no longer saw anything. Just trees swaying in the breeze and branches scattered in every direction. She squinted, peering into the tree line. The other day, she could have sworn she saw a stray gray dog trotting past the window at the Grille. But when she'd gone outside to try to lure it indoors, it had been nowhere to be found. Sometimes she wondered if she was seeing things.

Amanda turned and held her breath, bracing herself as she pushed through the building's glass double doors. Thankfully, the inside of the shelter seemed to have fared much better than the outside. Other than a few buckets placed strategically around the lobby to catch rainwater, things looked generally the same as they had when she'd shown up for her volunteer shift last week. Just damper, although the industrial-sized fan whirring in the corner seemed to be doing its best to dry things out.

"Afternoon, Amanda." Hans Bennett, the shelter volunteer manning the front desk, waved and called out to her above the hum of the fan.

"Hi, Hans." She waved back, and as she approached the counter, she spotted a kitten nestled in Hans's lap.

Of course.

In the epic dogs versus cats question, the older gentleman was firmly on the side of the felines. Since he'd retired and doubled down on his volunteer hours at the shelter, he'd become a virtual hero every kitten season when the shelter was always bursting with frail, furry bodies that needed to be bottle-fed round the clock.

"Who've you got there?" she asked, nodding toward the little ginger tabby napping on Hans's khakis.

"This here's Lucille Ball." He grinned and rubbed the tip of his pointer finger along the kitten's tiny cheek.

"Lucille Ball? Cute. Let me guess—Birdie and Bunny let you name her." Hans was nothing if not nostalgic for times gone by. He was the president of the Spring Forest Historical Society and had a thorough knowledge of the area's involvement in the Underground Railroad back during the Civil War. Amanda couldn't help having a soft spot for him.

"They did. As I'm sure you can tell, they've got their hands pretty full at the moment." He cast a knowing glance at the ceiling.

Amanda followed his gaze and shook her head. "This is bad. Has the insurance company sent anyone out to take a look?"

Hans shrugged. "Not yet."

That seemed strange. Seven days was a long time. Then again, the storm damage spread to Raleigh and beyond. The area insurance adjusters were probably working overtime. "Let's hope they get someone out here soon. The shelter can't go on like this indefinitely. Speaking of which, how's Tucker? Have you seen him?"

"I have, and he's as cantankerous as ever." The older man rolled his eyes, then reached for the phone when it started to ring.

Amanda mouthed *see you later* as he launched into a conversation with someone who sounded like a potential pet parent. She breathed a little easier as she headed down the long hallway leading toward the kennel area. If Tucker was cranky, he was more than likely fine. If he'd become cuddly overnight, she'd really have something to worry about.

A few more carefully arranged buckets caught dripping water in the kennel area even though it wasn't even raining outside, which didn't bode well for whatever was going on in the attic. But Amanda couldn't help but smile as all but one of the dogs darted to the front of their enclosures to greet her with yips and wagging tails.

"Hi, guys." She greeted each pup by name until she reached the last kennel on the left, where the one holdout was tucked into a ball in the corner with his eyes closed and his head resting on his paws.

"Hello to you too, Grumpy." She unlatched the door to Tucker's enclosure, walked inside and crouched down in front of the stubborn little dog. "You're not fooling me. I know you're not asleep. Your paws always twitch when you nap for real."

As if on cue, Tucker opened one disinterested eye.

Amanda reached into her pocket and pulled out a few crumbles of goat cheese—leftovers from her experimental puff pastry. She held them out in an open palm and whispered, "I brought you a present, but don't tell the others."

Tucker's tiny nose twitched, then his other eye sprang open and he lifted his head. But in true grumpy form, he picked gently at the cheese instead of gulping it down like a normal stray dog would, as if he was doing her a favor by eating it.

"Why you're my favorite is a mystery I'll never understand," Amanda muttered.

Then, much to her irritation, Ryan Carter's perfectly irritable, perfectly handsome face popped into her consciousness. She sighed. Damn him, and damn his chiseled bone structure.

"You know what they say about women who are attracted to dark and brooding characters, don't you?" a familiar voice behind her asked.

Amanda scooped Tucker into her arms and turned around to find Birdie Whitaker smiling blithely at her from the other side of the chain-link gate. "Hi, Birdie. And no, I don't know that they say. But I have a feeling you're about to tell me."

Of course she was. Birdie never hesitated to speak her mind. "Scientists say it indicates a primal desire to find a strong, virile man who can give you lots of healthy babies."

Amanda could feel tiny beads of sweat forming on her brow.

"That's the craziest thing I've ever heard." Beyond crazy. She didn't have time for even one baby, much less a lot of them. "Besides, Tucker is a dog. Not a man."

Ryan was a man, though. And whether she wanted to admit it or not, she was definitely attracted to him. But Birdie didn't need to know that. No one did.

The older woman shrugged. "True, but you're the only one who seems to appreciate his less-than-sparkling personality. Are you saying you wouldn't like him if he were a human being?"

She held Tucker a little closer to her heart. "That's not what I'm saying at all. But he's not. He's a dog, and I'm not ready for any children. Or a husband. So something about your scientific study must be flawed."

"You're probably right. What do they know? They're just scientists." Birdie bit back a smile. "Like Einstein and his ilk."

Amanda rolled her eyes.

What had gotten into everyone? There hadn't been this much interest in her nonexistent love life in… well…*ever*. "People are acting strange. I'm beginning to wonder if the storm blew in more than just the tornado."

"The tornado was plenty. I think the storm might have rattled everyone." Birdie looked around and sighed. "It sure rattled this old building."

It had to be heartbreaking for Birdie to see the shelter in such bad shape. Neither she nor her sister had ever married. Bunny had been engaged once, years ago, but Birdie never talked about her past relationships. Every time the subject came up, she said her heart belonged to the animals at Furever Paws.

Amanda carried Tucker out of the kennel, shut the gate behind her and gave Birdie a hug with her free arm. "It's going to be okay. As soon as the insurance money comes in, you can get someone out here to do repairs and everything will be as good as new."

Ever stoic, Birdie nodded. "You're right. This shelter has been here almost twenty years, and we've saved hundreds of animals, from dogs and cats to llamas and goats. It's going to take more than a tornado to stop us."

"Exactly." Amanda nodded. "You and Bunny know I'll help in any way I can, right?"

"Of course we do, dear." Birdie's gaze shifted to the dog in Amanda's arms. "Are you going to walk that prickly little beast, or do you want to hear more about that scientific study I mentioned?"

"Nice try." Amanda laughed. "But there's a patch of grass with Tucker's name on it outside."

"See you later, sugar," Birdie said in her Carolina drawl that Amanda knew so well, but when she smiled it didn't quite reach her eyes.

Amanda carried Tucker out back and didn't set him down on the ground until they'd crossed the gravel lot and reached the sprawling emerald lawn that led to the old Victorian farmhouse where the Whitaker sisters had lived all their lives. Tucker didn't like walking on gravel. Or dirt. Or pretty much anything other than soft grass. Amanda didn't feel like playing tug-of-war with him on his leash today, so she indulged the dog once she'd put him down and let him drag her around the yard with his nose to the ground while she took in more damage from the storm.

There were a few more downed trees closer to Birdie and Bunny's house, and the portable storage sheds behind the shelter had taken a beating. One of them was lying on its side, which probably meant that the dog food it housed had been ruined.

What a mess.

"It'll be fine, though," she said to Tucker. "No one got hurt. That's the most important thing, right?"

It was like talking to a brick wall. The little dog completely ignored her, because of course he did.

Birdie was crazy if she thought that's the kind of

man Amanda wanted to end up with someday. It was one thing to willingly hang out with a standoffish dog, but marrying an actual person who acted in such a way would be insane. Take Ryan Carter, for instance. Just when he'd finally acknowledged her existence and complimented her coffee, he upped and switched back into his indifferent self and bolted. He'd practically sprinted away from her, right there on Main Street. It would have been mortifying, if she cared about how he treated her.

Which she absolutely did *not*.

Tucker cocked his head at her, and she must have been imagining things because she could have sworn he had a mocking little gleam in his eyes, as if he knew exactly what—or whom—she was thinking about.

She glared at him. "Don't start."

She needed to get him back to his kennel anyway, or else she wouldn't have time to walk any of the other dogs before she had to return to the Grille for the dinner rush. So she scooped him into her arms and made her way back to the kennel area.

She didn't mean to overhear Birdie and Bunny's conversation. She really didn't. They were speaking in such hushed tones that at first Amanda thought she was alone in the concrete room. But as she rounded the corner toward the row of enclosures where Tucker's kennel was located, their soft, Southern drawls grew louder. More urgent.

"I don't understand," Bunny said. "Twenty thousand dollars? Out of our own pockets? We don't have that kind of money."

"We'll just have get it somehow." Birdie's tone was flat. Determined.

She'd always been the more practical sister—a no-nonsense go-getter, while Bunny was more of a dreamer. Sweet as could be, but somewhat naive.

Bunny sighed. "But what about the insurance?"

Amanda cleared her throat. She needed to make her presence known before she heard something she shouldn't. But the sisters didn't seem to hear her, too caught up in their intense conversation.

"Oh Bunny, that's what I'm trying to tell you." Birdie's voice cracked, and it was then that Amanda realized it was too late. Too late to interrupt. Too late to pretend she hadn't just realized the shelter was in serious trouble. "We don't *have* any insurance."

Chapter Three

"We're out of the pulled pork and hush puppies special," Amanda poked her head into the dining room and announced.

"That was quick." Belle glanced at her watch and sighed.

The Grille wasn't scheduled to close for another two hours, and now they were down to one special—the pot roast. Slow-simmered in beef broth and smothered in onion gravy, it wasn't bad. But it wasn't nearly as good as the wine-based recipe Amanda had been experimenting with.

Last week she'd brought her newest creation along to Sunday dinner at her parents' house and placed it on the table as if it were a foil-wrapped work of art, steeped in pinot noir and slender, woodsy porcini mushrooms.

Her sister and brother-in-law had loved it, as had her brother, Josh. Even her nieces and nephews had given it glowing reviews. But she hadn't been able to convince her parents that it should replace the pot roast recipe the Grille had been using for the past sixty-eight years. They'd gone on and on about tradition and down-home Southern cooking, as if she'd told them she wanted to start feeding the good people of Spring Forest foie gras. It was maddening.

Amanda was trying her best to be patient. Her mom, in particular, had been especially sensitive about changing anything at the Grille since Amanda's grandmother passed away last year. The restaurant had become a sort of monument.

But it couldn't stay the same *forever*, could it? If this was going to be Amanda's life from here on out, she needed to be able to put her own stamp on it.

But tonight, for once, she hadn't spent the better part of the dinner rush rewriting the Grille's menu in her head. While she'd been busy taking tickets from Belle, calling out orders to the kitchen staff and plating one serving of pulled pork after another, her mind had been back at Furever Paws.

How was it possible that Birdie and Bunny didn't have insurance? It didn't make sense. Amanda was pretty sure their younger brother, Gator, took care of all the shelter's business dealings. And Gator was a big shot investment banker or something like that. He lived in a fancy Antebellum-style mansion outside Durham, with huge white columns and a yard full of trees dripping with Spanish moss. The house was so grand it had been pictured in *Southern Living* a few years ago. With all of his business success, and the many investments he'd made over the years, surely he knew the importance of having property insurance.

Then again, it didn't really matter *why* the shelter was uninsured. The most important thing now was finding the money elsewhere to fix the storm damage, and apparently it was going to cost twenty thousand dollars. Minimum.

She wiped her hands on a dish towel and headed to the dining room to correct the specials board with her head in a fog, trying to come up with a way to help that didn't involve admitting to Birdie and Bunny she'd overheard their private conversation. But again, twenty thousand dollars was a lot of money. An enormous amount. If Amanda had that kind of cash just sitting around, she'd have already launched her dream catering add-on at the Grille. There was no way she could solve their problem on her own, and bringing in other people would mean sharing their secret.

At the moment, she had more pressing problems because no sooner had she climbed the step stool and swiped the eraser across the words *pulled pork barbecue sandwich with hush puppies* on the chalkboard hanging on the wall just to the right of the pie safe than someone behind her let out a sigh.

"Looks like I'm too late for the barbecue."

Amanda turned to find Dr. Richard Jackson looking up at her with his arms crossed and a furrow in his brow.

"Sorry, Doc. We're clean out." Amanda stepped

down until her feet were once again planted firmly on the Grille's white-and-black-tiled floor. "You're here a little later than usual, aren't you?"

Dr. Jackson had become a regular at the Grille shortly after his wife passed away five years ago. Now he was almost like family and he usually showed up for dinner at six fifteen sharp, right after his veterinary practice closed up shop for the night.

He shrugged and did a little head tilt that made him look even more like Denzel Washington than he normally did. "I was out helping Birdie and Bunny with a sick llama."

Amanda frowned. "Which one? Drama or Llama Bean?"

"Llama Bean." He waved a hand. "Don't worry—she's going to be fine."

"That was sweet of you." Amanda lifted a brow.

Doc J was spending more and more time volunteering his services at Furever Paws, and she couldn't help but wonder if he was interested in one of the Whitaker sisters. She just couldn't figure out which one. Then again, maybe the additional volunteering was only because his schedule wasn't quite as packed as usual since his daughter, Lauren, was set to take over his practice at the end of the year.

But something about the twinkle in his eyes told her he was thinking about more than just a sick llama. "It was nothing, really. Just a mild ear infection."

"Nonsense. I'm sure Birdie and Bunny really appreciate all you do for them. I was out there earlier today too. We must have just missed each other."

"I guess we did. Did you see the storm damage? Such a shame." The older man's smile dimmed somewhat, but he still looked as handsome as ever. At sixty-seven, he was just a few years older than both Birdie and Bunny, who were ages sixty-four and sixty-three. He'd be a perfect match for either sister.

Not that she should be meddling in the Whitaker sisters' personal lives, even though Birdie had most definitely taken an interest in Amanda's.

"The roof needs some major repairs. I'm toying with the idea of throwing them a fundraiser. I'm just trying to get everything figured out before I talk to Birdie and Bunny about it." She bit her lip. "I wonder how profitable a bake sale could be."

Twenty thousand dollars translated into a massive amount of brownies and cupcakes, but so far it was the only thing she'd come up with.

"I'm sure every little bit would help." Doc J cast a longing glance at the plateful of pulled pork on Belle's tray as she shuffled past them. "But you might raise more money if you held a barbecue instead."

He laughed. So did Amanda, until the wheels in her head starting turning.

She knew a lot of pit masters in the area. What if she could get a few of them together, all on the same day? They could make a real event of it. Maybe Birdie and Bunny could set up an adoption booth with some of the dogs and cats from the shelter. And maybe Amanda could ask some of the other local businesses to set up booths. She could organize a whole festival, all centered around a barbecue cook-off.

"I know you're just kidding, but that might actually work. You're a genius, Doc." She beamed at him. "Tonight's dinner is on me. Okay?"

"I'm not turning down a free dinner. Bring me whatever you recommend." He winked and slid into a booth facing Main Street.

"One pot roast special, coming right up." She turned toward the kitchen, mind reeling.

The more she thought about it, the more a barbecue cook-off seemed like the perfect idea for a fundraiser. Now she just needed to make some calls to the pit masters she knew—a few food truck operators in Raleigh, plus some of the college barbecue hangouts in Wilmington. Once she had at least three on board, she'd present the idea to Birdie and Bunny.

"You look awfully happy all of a sudden." Belle looked up from assembling a to-go order on the sleek stainless steel counter just inside the kitchen's swinging door. "Has anything in particular put that giddy expression on your face?"

"Maybe." Amanda bit back a smile. Best not to say anything until she was certain she could pull it off.

"Since you're in such a chipper mood, can you take these out front while I grab a pitcher of sweet tea?" Belle offered her two white paper bags, all sealed up and ready to go.

Amanda took them. "The last of the pulled pork, I presume?"

"Yes, they go to the father and son waiting by the register. He's already paid." Belle focused intently on the pitcher in her hands, almost as if she were afraid of dropping it. Which was something Belle never, ever did.

Odd.

But Amanda didn't have time to figure out what was going on with Belle. They were still in the middle of the dinner rush, plus she might have a fundraiser to plan. "When you get a chance, Doc J needs an order of the pot roast. On the house."

"I'm on it, boss," Belle said, again without meeting her gaze.

Amanda shook her head as she pushed her way through the swinging door, but as soon as she was on the other side, the reason for Belle's strange behavior was clear.

Ryan Carter stood waiting at the counter, presumably for the bags in Amanda's hands. But unlike all the previous times he'd been to the Grille, he wasn't alone. A little boy around five or six years old stood beside him, clutching a bright red dinosaur toy with one hand and Ryan's big palm with the other. There was a sadness in the child's eyes that made Amanda's heart feel like it was being squeezed in a vise, a sadness that also made her think twice about the reasons behind Ryan's ever-present scowl.

She smiled at the boy, and his gaze dropped quickly to the ground. So she had no choice but to focus on his father, standing just a few feet away and looking like the world's most handsome single dad, scowl notwithstanding. She wished she had something to stare at other than his strong jaw and rugged face. She wished it so hard that her hands grew sweaty and the to-go bags nearly fell to the ground.

"You again." She set the paper bags on the counter and without thinking, wiped her damp palms on her frilly gingham apron. Definitely not the most attractive move she could have made, but he'd caught her off guard. She could hardly think straight. *Belle is totally fired.* "Welcome back."

The corner of his mouth twitched, as if he was trying his best to smile but had forgotten how. "Thank you. It's good to see you. I'm glad you haven't suffered any permanent injuries from our earlier run-in."

He remembered her.

Finally.

Of course he remembers. He nearly mowed you down on the sidewalk. Don't read too much into it. "Nope. I'm still all in one piece."

"Good to know."

Other than their awkward sidewalk collision, this was the closest Amanda had ever been to Ryan Carter. Since he hadn't plowed into her this time, she was free to examine him without the distraction of an aching nose. He had the nicest eyes she'd ever seen—golden brown with a ring of deep amber in the center. Rich and pure, like Carolina honey drizzled on a biscuit.

She felt woozy all of a sudden, as if she'd been sipping the whiskey she kept on hand for her special bread pudding sauce.

"Well," she said, and gestured to the bags.

That was his cue to leave. She much preferred crushing on the swoonworthy newspaperman from afar. Up close, he was far too intense. Far too dangerous, if the sudden pounding of her heart was any indication.

She wasn't good at the whole flirting and dating thing. The one time she'd put herself out there and asked someone on a date, she'd been so nervous that she'd vomited on the boy's feet immediately after she'd gotten the words out. It had been mortifying, obviously. Amanda still couldn't bring herself to talk about it, even when Belle urged her to try to move past "the Sadie Hawkins incident." It had become part of the town lore, and according to one of Amanda's nieces, kids at Spring Forest High *still* talked about it.

No matter. Amanda had no intention of flirting with Ryan. The very idea of going on a date with the man terrified her, and she definitely didn't have time for it, especially if she was going to put together a massive fundraiser on top of her already jam-packed schedule.

Just go away, she wanted to say. *Go away and let me catch my breath.*

She didn't say it, of course. And he clearly wasn't a mind reader because he didn't budge. He just kept looking at her while her knees went weak.

Why is this so hard?

It wasn't as if she'd never gone on a date before. She'd dated…a little. But she'd never had a serious relationship, mainly because she liked to keep men at arm's length. As the only biracial woman in Spring Forest— other than her sister, obviously—dating could be complicated. She'd been called *striking* or told that her looks were *unusual* more times than she could count.

Oddly enough, her brother, Josh, didn't seem to have

that problem. Or maybe he simply didn't let it get to him. All Amanda knew was that he dated all the time, which would have been a nightmare in and of itself. She wouldn't be able to cope with Sadie Hawkins–type nerves on such a regular basis.

No. Way.

Maybe it would have been easier if she lived in a big city like Raleigh or Charlotte—somewhere more metropolitan. But her family had roots here. The Grille itself was a reminder that the Sylvesters had been in Spring Forest for generations. Amanda was happy in her hometown.

She just found it much simpler to go it alone.

Amanda gripped the edge of the counter and smiled at the little boy, who had the same striking eyes as his father. "What's your name, sweetie?"

He tightened his grip on his triceratops until his little knuckles went white.

"This is Dillon," Ryan said. "Barbecue is his favorite. I usually try to pick up our dinner on my way home, but thought he could use an outing, so here we are."

Here they were indeed.

"Is that right? Is barbecue really your favorite?" She moved around the counter and crouched down so she was on eye level with Dillon.

Her effort earned her a nod and a tiny hint of a smile.

"Of course it is." Ryan gave his son's hand a squeeze, and there was a new tenderness in his tone that did nothing to help the weak-in-the-knees situation. "We never lie about barbecue, do we, bud?"

He'd mirrored his words from this afternoon.

I never lie about coffee.

Cute.

Way too cute. Adorable, actually.

"Hot dogs are the only thing I cook that he's interested in eating. Even single fathers know kids can't eat hot dogs seven nights a week." Ryan's smile turned sheepish.

Why did he seem even more attractive now that she knew he was a single dad? All he needed now was a puppy in his arms and she'd be a goner.

But the thought of puppies reminded her of Tucker, which in turn reminded her that she was supposed to be making calls to pit masters to help the shelter, not standing around mooning over her secret crush and his bashful mini-me.

She stood and nudged the paper bags closer to him. "I hope you enjoy it."

He took the hint this time and reached for the food. "We will. Thank you…" His usual unreadable expression gave way to one of befuddlement—charming Hugh Grant–style befuddlement, because of course. "I didn't catch your name."

"Amanda." Out of the corner of her eye, she saw Belle refilling the coffeepot just a few feet away, looking pleased as punch. "Amanda Sylvester."

He nodded. "Have a good evening, Amanda Sylvester."

And then he was gone, only instead of walking down Main Street with his signature brisk pace and ramrod-straight spine, he matched his steps with Dillon's and rested one of his big hands on the little boy's shoulder.

Amanda's heart gave a tiny squeeze.

She ignored it as best she could and swiveled to face Belle. "You did that on purpose. You knew I was distracted, so you caught me off guard and had me come out here to deliver his dinner."

Belle grinned from ear to ear. "Of course I did, but look on the bright side. At least now you know he's not married."

Amanda almost wished she wasn't privy to that fascinating bit of information. "It doesn't matter. I'm not looking for a boyfriend, remember?"

Or, God forbid, a husband. While Amanda struggled in the small-town dating world, her sister married the first boy who'd ever asked her out. Alexis and Paul had gotten engaged right out of high school and look what had happened. She'd had six kids in eight years and no longer had time to brush her teeth, much less run a business.

No, thank you.

Amanda loved her nieces and nephews, but every time she babysat for them, the night ended in some kind of disaster. Under her watch, Alexis and Paul's living room walls had been "decorated" in permanent marker and their toilet had been plugged up with stuffed animals. How was it easier to walk six dogs than it was to supervise the same number of rambunctious children?

"His son is awfully cute, though. Don't you think?" Belle arched an eyebrow.

Yes, she definitely thought so. He had such a quiet

way about him. So serious, just like his dad. Something about the way he'd held on so tightly to his red
dinosaur made her want to cook up some comfort food
for him. Macaroni and cheese, topped with a thick
layer of toasted bread crumbs, maybe—followed by
a creamy coconut pie. Her nieces and nephews loved
her coconut pie.

She glanced at Belle who was watching her as if she
knew exactly what Amanda was thinking.

"Stop looking at me like that." She rolled her eyes,
but Belle's grin widened, so she added, "You're fired
again, by the way."

Belle winked. "I think the words you're looking for
are *thank you*."

"Look at that." Ryan pointed his fork at the empty
plate sitting in front of Dillon. "You ate every bite."

His son nodded and smiled a crooked smile that hit
Ryan dead in the center of his chest.

He hadn't been flirting when he'd told Amanda Sylvester that barbecue was Dillon's favorite food. It was
the truth. He'd simply been carrying on a normal conversation. It didn't have to mean anything, and it definitely didn't have to mean that he found her attractive
or that the gentle way she'd spoken to Dillon had made
him feel oddly emotional for some reason.

Except he *did* find her attractive, and the soothing
tone of her voice as she'd talked to his son had done
something to him—something strange and calming.
For a split second, his worries had slipped away and
he'd felt like maybe, just maybe, everything would be

okay. Which meant flirting with her hadn't been mean-
ingless, although he didn't want to think about that
right now. He wanted to enjoy the unexpected light-
ness he'd felt as he'd left the Main Street Grille. Hell,
he would have bottled that feeling if he could.

"Want some of mine?" Ryan slid his plate toward
Dillon.

The boy shook his head. His face and hands were
sticky with barbecue sauce, as was the red dinosaur
toy, which was now standing on the table, poised to
strike at Dillon's half-full glass of milk.

Ryan's in-laws would have been horrified. Annabelle and Finch Brewster would never have allowed
Dillon to bring a toy to the table, and the head shake
would have been deemed wholly unacceptable.

*Say "no, thank you." Where are your manners, Dil-
lon?*

Ryan could practically hear the voice of Maggie's
mother in his head. No matter how many times he'd
told Annabelle and Finch about what the child psychol-
ogist had recommended about not trying to force Dillon to speak, they continued to press him about *please*
and *thank you*, *yes sir* and *no ma'am*.

It irritated Ryan to no end. He was doing everything he could to protect his son's fragile emotional
state, and whenever they were around, they sabotaged
him at every turn. Sometimes he felt like it was inten-
tional, like they were trying to prevent him from fully
bonding with Dillon.

Surely that wasn't true. Annabelle and Finch were
Dillon's grandparents, and in their own dysfunctional

way, they loved him. Ryan did his best to chalk their misplaced interference up to grief. Maggie had been their only child.

But they were also lifelong members of the country club set, so their world revolved around appearances and social niceties. They'd liked Ryan better when he was a political editor at one of the most esteemed newspapers in the country instead of a journalistic one-man show in the Deep South. And sadly, they'd liked their grandson better back then too. They acted as if his refusal to talk was a form of rebellion. Couldn't they see he was grieving?

"How about a movie before you wash up and get ready for bed? *Lion King?*" It was one of the few things Dillon liked better than barbecue. He knew every line and every song of the movie by heart, and sometimes Ryan liked to put it on just so he could watch his son's lips move, mouthing the words—times like tonight, when happiness seemed almost close enough to touch.

Ryan didn't want to think about Amanda's part in making him feel that way. He just wanted to enjoy the faint stirring of hope before it slipped away. But as Dillon climbed down from his chair and carried his dinosaur to the den, Ryan's new phone rang, punctuating the hopeful silence with a grating reminder that nothing had changed. Not yet anyway. A newsman couldn't ignore a call. *The Spring Forest Chronicle* was a far cry from the *Post*, but Ryan was the editor-in-chief. He had a responsibility to his job, just like he had back in DC.

He glanced down at his cell, where Annabelle and

Finch's contact information lit up the small screen. Of course.

His thumb hovered over the green Accept button, but he couldn't bring himself to answer the call. The conversation would be the same as it always was—awkward small talk, followed by a request to talk to Dillon. Once again, Ryan would have to admit that his son still wasn't speaking.

No.

Just…

No.

Not tonight. He'd deal with Maggie's parents later. For now, he'd watch a movie with his son, and if his thoughts wandered every so often to Amanda Sylvester, her bright smile and the subtle sprinkle of freckles across her rich complexion, then so be it.

Why fight it?

There was no harm in thinking about her when nothing whatsoever would come of it. Other than brief interactions at the Grille, he had no intention of seeing her again. Even if he wanted to, he couldn't. There was no room in his life whatsoever for a relationship—not even with a woman who made him want things he hadn't even thought about in months…maybe even years. Things he wouldn't, *couldn't* have.

At least that's what Ryan told himself as he followed Dillon into the other room and let the call roll to voice mail.

Chapter Four

"Tell me about the night the tornado came through." Ryan's pen was poised above the reporter's notebook in the palm of his hand as he glanced back and forth between Birdie and Bunny Whitaker, waiting for a response.

The dishes from his barbecue dinner the night before were still sitting in the sink, right where he'd left them. He and Dillon had fallen asleep on the floor in front of the television somewhere around the point when a grown-up Simba reunited with Nala. Ryan had woken up this morning in a tangle of blankets with Dillon's head on his shoulder, and he'd been reluctant to move, despite the nagging pain in his back. One of these days, he really needed to start sleeping in a bed again.

Back spasms aside, he'd let his son sleep as long as

he could before finally relenting and waking him up for a quick bath and breakfast in time for school. It had been a good morning—the best in a long while. The dishes could wait.

Ryan was tempted to believe that Amanda Sylvester had something to do with his good mood, but he stopped short of embracing the notion. They'd only exchanged a handful of words. She probably didn't even remember their interactions. He was a customer, no different from all the others.

To help put an end to his ridiculous fantasies, he'd skipped his usual trip to the Grille for morning coffee and gone straight to the office, where Jonah had handed him a message from Furever Paws and a cup of instant, undrinkable coffee that he hadn't been able to make himself choke down, no matter how badly he needed it.

And now here he stood—under-caffeinated, back aching—interviewing the Whitaker sisters while a sick llama gave him some serious side-eye.

Birdie, the taller and more stoic of the two, was the first to answer his question. She launched into a detailed rundown of the night in question, starting with moving all the special needs dogs and cats into the basement of the farmhouse she shared with her sister.

The old clapboard Victorian loomed behind her while the three of them looked out at the paddock beyond the garden gate where a few farm animals dozed in the morning sun—a handful of sheep, pigs and goats, plus a milk cow and another llama named Drama. For some reason, Drama's partner, Llama Bean, had taken an intense interest in Ryan. She craned her long neck, sniffing the lapel of his Armani suit jacket as he tried not to flinch.

Birdie continued, "We just did our best to ride it out, and didn't realize quite how bad we'd been hit until the next morning when it was safe to go back outside."

Ryan's gaze flitted briefly to Llama Bean. She made a humming noise, which he desperately hoped was a happy sound. "How did the animals do throughout the night?"

"The poor dears were terrified." Bunny shook her head. "Just thinking about it again breaks my heart. The whole ordeal was so scary that I've had nightmares about it almost every night. I think I have PMS."

Ryan's pen froze midscribble.

"She means PTSD." Birdie rolled her eyes.

"Noted." Ryan cleared his throat.

"We were lucky, really. We were all seriously rattled, but no one was hurt. A couple of our volunteers hunkered down in the shelter basement with the animals we couldn't move to the house. Matt Fielding and Claire Asher came out of nowhere and kept the barn animals safe." Was it Ryan's imagination, or did the llama puff out its chest a little at the mention of the barn animals? "Once we had a chance to survey the damage, we found a stray dog pinned under one of the downed trees. Luckily, Matt was able to free her. He even ended up adopting her. We're happy to say she's recovering nicely in her new home."

"Hope should be the flower girl in Matt and Claire's wedding, don't you think?" Bunny exhaled a dreamy sigh.

Ryan's eyes narrowed. "Who's Hope?"

"The dog, obviously," Bunny said.

"Yes." He suppressed a grin. This was supposed to be a serious interview, after all. "Obviously."

Birdie crossed her arms. "You don't need to include the flower girl part in the article. But perhaps you'd like to see the spot where we found the injured dog?"

Ryan nodded, game for anything that put more distance between himself and Llama Bean, whose humming noises had morphed into a clucking sound. He took a backward step and the animal's ears flattened against her head.

Bunny patted his forearm. "Don't worry about the llama, dear. She's just flirting with you."

"Super," he deadpanned.

"Come this way." Birdie motioned for him to follow, and he acquiesced, shoving his notepad in the inside pocket of his jacket and pulling out his iPhone.

The display still showed last night's missed call notification from Maggie's parents, along with an alert that they'd left a voice mail. He made the reminders vanish with swipes of his thumb before accessing the phone's camera.

The Whitaker sisters continued showing him around, pausing every so often for one of their quirky exchanges that Ryan found more entertaining than anything he'd witnessed on the political beat in Washington. He snapped photographs of the worst of the tornado damage, which was far more extensive than anything he'd seen in town. "I'm glad you called. Our readers will definitely be interested in what went on around here during the storm, especially the part about Hope's rescue."

Everyone loved a feel-good story. And compared to most of the news pieces he'd penned lately, this one had feature-story potential. The people and animals at Furever Paws had been through a harrowing ordeal, but they'd survived—and had even saved another animal in the process. Although it had happened a week ago, he might even be able to make room for it on the front page, given the scarcity of hard-hitting news in Spring Forest.

"So you're really going to write about us?" Bunny asked, clapping her hands as they came to a stop in the gravel driveway of the main shelter building.

"Absolutely." He nodded and took a picture of the Furever Paws logo painted on the front of the shelter—a cat and dog silhouetted inside a curved heart—with the damaged roof visible off to the side.

"Thank you, Mr. Carter." Bunny beamed at him. "Thank you *so* much."

Birdie held up a finger. "Would it be possible to include something specific in your article?"

Ryan pocketed his phone and reached for his notepad again. "That depends. What might this 'something specific' be?"

The sisters exchanged a glance, and Birdie took a deep breath. "The reason we called you out here is that we're hoping you can not only highlight the damage done to the shelter, but that you might also call on the community to attend our barbecue fundraiser for all the repair work."

He looked up from his pad while visions of Amanda

swirled in his consciousness. The tangy taste of her barbecue sauce seemed to linger on his tongue.

Barbecue fundraiser?

It was a coincidence. It had to be. "You're having a community event to raise money for the shelter?"

"Yes. As you can see, we're in desperate need of a new roof, and the fact of the matter is that we don't have the money to pay for it. One of our most devoted dog walkers called this morning to tell us she'd like to plan a big barbecue cook-off."

"Is that so?" Ryan tugged at his shirt collar. The thought of Amanda had made him instantly warm, which was absurd. He was a grown man, not some love-sick teenager. "Does this philanthropic dog walker have a name?"

"Amanda Sylvester," Birdie said. *Of course.* "Maybe you've met her—she runs the Main Street Grille. Very pretty girl. Smart, too."

"And single," Bunny chimed in.

Ryan stared at them both. Were they mind readers? Or did he seem completely desperate for female companionship?

The latter. Had to be.

"Anyway." Birdie smiled sweetly at him. A little too sweetly, maybe. "Amanda reached out to a few folks last night and, already, pit masters from all over the state have agreed to come. Plus, she's hoping to get some local businesses to sponsor booths with games and raffles. A feature on the event would really help us get the turnout we're hoping for. That way, we can raise the funds we need to pay for the repairs."

"I'd be happy to mention the fundraiser in the article. You have my contact information—give me a call or send an email to let me know the details of when and where this event will take place once you have it finalized. Thank you for your time." He nodded and headed to his vehicle. For once, he had no trouble identifying it, probably because it was the only automobile in the small lot without a Furever Paws sticker proudly displayed on its back window.

By the time he paused, he'd already grasped the door handle. Ryan wasn't sure what made him turn around and ask one more question. He had plenty of information to put together a feature article.

Still…

A proper journalist would take the time to speak to the person in charge of the fundraiser before writing about it. And if Ryan Carter was anything, he was first and foremost an ethical newsman. Which was the only logical explanation for what came next.

"Should I arrange a time to chat with Miss Sylvester about the barbecue cook-off?" He swallowed. Hard. "For the article, I mean."

The sisters exchanged a bemused glance.

"I think that's a wonderful idea." Birdie cleared her throat. "For the article."

Ryan nodded. "Excellent. I'll give her a call and set something up."

For the article.

Who was he kidding?

He wasn't even sure he believed it himself.

* * *

Belle looked Amanda up and down as she poured herself a cup of coffee Friday morning and shook her head. "That's what you're wearing?"

"Hello to you, too." Amanda arched a brow and took a deep, fortifying gulp of Appalachian Breakfast Blend, one of the custom coffees she picked up regularly from a microroaster just outside Asheville. As morning blends went, it was a strong one.

But was it strong enough to make up for the night she'd just spent tossing and turning at the thought of being interviewed by Ryan Carter today? Doubtful.

"Hello, good morning and all that jazz. But seriously." Belle slung her purse on the counter and cast a pointed glance at Amanda's Main Street Grille T-shirt and skinny jeans. "That's what you're wearing for your lunch date?"

She knew she shouldn't have told Belle about her meeting with Ryan, although it wasn't like she could keep it a secret since they were meeting at the Grille. She supposed she could have asked him to move the interview down the street to *The Spring Forest Chronicle* office, but if she had to have an extended one-on-one conversation with the man, she preferred it take place on her turf. She felt comfortable at the Grille. If she accidentally started flirting with him again, the odds of tossing her cookies on his designer shoes seemed much smaller.

She was steering clear of breakfast though. Better to be safe than sorry.

"It's not a date. Why would you think that?" She busied herself with opening the register for the day so she wouldn't have to look Belle in the eye. She didn't think her best friend would be able to see inside her head and know that she'd tried on three different dresses before giving up and settling on her ordinary work uniform, but she couldn't be sure.

What was wrong with her Main Street Grille T-shirt, anyway? It was a cute shade of Carolina blue and had a little ruffle at the bottom of the sleeves—a definite upgrade from the dingy burgundy T-shirt she'd worn when she washed dishes at the Grille in high school. More importantly, it was *appropriate*. Because her lunch with Ryan Carter was *not* a date.

Not even close.

"Not a date? Are you sure about that? Horrific wardrobe choices aside, your lips are cherry red. That's the new lipstick you bought last month at Sephora during our girls' trip to Raleigh." Belle's gaze flitted to Amanda's feet and she gasped. "Oh! And you're wearing your cute flats with the little daisies on them. Total date shoes."

Damn her whimsical footwear.

"Are they too much?" She glanced down at the ballerina flats. They were, weren't they? She should change into something less feminine. Less pretty. Less...*everything*.

"No, they're not too much. Neither is the lipstick. I'm trying to tell you that you look gorgeous—as gorgeous as you possibly can while wearing that T-shirt. Mr. Hot Single Dad won't be able to take his eyes off you."

"Don't call him that. Please." In her head, she still called him Mr. Cranky Pants. Although lately, he'd been a tad less stilted than usual. Still, it suited him. When he'd called to arrange the interview, he'd sounded as formal and businesslike as if he'd been setting up a meeting with the queen of England.

Amanda frowned into her coffee. "And I'm quite certain he'll be able to take his eyes off me. He shouldn't be looking at me at all. He should be taking notes or something, shouldn't he? This meeting isn't about me. It's about Furever Paws and the rescue animals and the fundraiser to help get the shelter back on its feet. It's *business*, and it most definitely *isn't* a date."

"Why can't it be both?"

"Because…" *Because I don't have time for a boyfriend. Because I'm trying to start a new business while running another one at the same time.* She swallowed. *Because how am I supposed to go on a date with him when simply talking to him turns me into a nervous wreck?* "Because it isn't, plain and simple."

She stomped to the door to flip the Closed sign over to the Open side. The daisy flats were already hurting her feet. Marvelous.

Belle opened her mouth to say something else, and Amanda held up a hand. "Can we stop talking about it, please?"

"If that's what you want."

Amanda nodded as she refilled her coffee cup. "It is."

"Okay, but can I say one more thing?" Belle folded her hands in a prayer position, so with no small amount of reluctance, Amanda nodded. "Your entire life re-

volves around responsibility. When you're not working at the Grille or whipping up new recipes for your
Instagram and planning your foodie takeover of Spring
Forest, you're volunteering at Furever Paws. And now
you're planning a massive fundraiser. You deserve to
have some fun every now and then."

"I have fun. Loads of it." It might have been a slight
exaggeration, but that was okay, wasn't it? Belle was
making it sound like Amanda's life was nothing but
drudgery and that simply wasn't true.

"Romantic fun?" Belle waited a beat for Amanda to
respond, but she refused, focusing instead on gathering
the ketchup bottles from the tables so she could refill
them before customers starting piling in. "I rest my
case. Come on, boss. I've watched you get all swoony
over this guy for weeks. This is your chance. If you
honestly think this isn't a date then you should ask
him out on a real one. *Today*. What's the worst that
could happen?"

Amanda whirled around to face her. "Seriously?"

Belle winked. "What are the odds it would happen
twice? A million to one?"

The bell on the front door chimed as Mollie McFadden walked in and headed toward one of the booths. As
usual, she had a dog in tow—a fluffy collie mix, this
time—but the sweet pup lowered into a down position
on the sidewalk just outside the door, waiting patiently
with its head resting on its paws.

Amanda had never been so happy to see a customer
before, especially Mollie. She ran a dog training busi-

ness, which would be a perfect fit for one of the booths at the barbecue cook-off.

"Good morning, Mollie." Amanda gave her a wave, then whispered to Belle, "Hand me a menu, would you? I'll take Mollie's order because I want to ask her about taking part in the fundraiser."

"Because that's easier than asking Ryan Carter out on a date?" Belle slid a menu off the stack near the register and offered it to her.

"You're fired." Amanda snatched it from her hands. "Again."

"You're weakening. I expected you to fire me ten minutes ago." Belle tied her apron around her waist with a satisfied flourish.

One of these days, Amanda was *really* going to fire her. Except she couldn't because she loved her too much.

The rest of the morning passed in a blur of activity. Mollie was thrilled to hear about Amanda's plans for the barbecue cook-off and happily agreed to run a booth at the event. The collie mix she was busy training for a client who lived in Raleigh never budged from his spot on the front walkway, and Amanda almost asked her if she could try transforming Tucker into a pet someone might actually want to take home, but she figured one favor was enough.

Still, by the time the breakfast rush was over, Amanda had served omelets and pancakes along with her sales pitch to several local business owners, each of whom had agreed to attend the fundraiser and man a booth. Even local farmer Cade Battle promised to show up and sell produce with his dad. It shouldn't have surprised her since he'd helped out the Whitaker sisters many times in the past. But somehow it still did, probably because Cade was cranky enough to make Tucker seem like the most likely pup to win the Miss Congeniality title in a dog show.

All in all, the plans for the barbecue cook-off were taking shape rapidly enough that she felt like she'd actually have something to talk about when Ryan showed up wearing one of his impeccably cut suits in all his perfectly posh glory.

Except the Ryan Carter who walked in the door five minutes before their scheduled appointment wasn't the Ryan Carter she'd been expecting. He was the same man, obviously—same piercing amber eyes, same charmingly rumpled hair, same broad shoulders. But for the first time since he'd blown into town like some strange and foreign treasure the tornado had dropped into her path, he wasn't wearing a coat and tie. Instead, his muscular form was covered in a cream-colored sweater and a pair of worn jeans.

She almost didn't believe her eyes.

Amanda blinked hard, wondering if she was seeing things. Or maybe Ryan had an identical twin she didn't know about. *Bryan* Carter, perhaps?

But then he aimed that intense, bone-melting gaze of his directly her way and she knew without a doubt that it was him. She'd know that stare anywhere. She took a shuddering inhale and tried not to ogle his chest, which was apparently more finely sculpted than it had looked under all those suits he'd been wearing. What was going on under that soft, luxe cashmere? He looked so good it was almost obscene.

The sweater appeared expensive—not to mention, soft as a baby kitten. Amanda wanted to bury her face in it and purr.

Oh God.

Maybe Belle was right. Maybe it *had* been too long since she'd been on a date.

"Hello." His mouth twitched into that almost-smiling thing he did sometimes, and her tummy flipped.

"Hi." Why did it feel like everyone in the diner was staring at her, waiting for her to be sick to her stomach?

Amanda glanced around. Everyone seemed much more focused on their burgers and club sandwiches than her awkward conversation. Even Belle was busy taking orders instead of spying on her.

Calm down.

She was fine. This was a simple interview for the paper, nothing more. "Shall we take a seat in one of the booths and chat about Furever Paws?"

"Sure." He motioned for her to lead the way.

She chose the booth in the farthest possible corner so they'd have a little privacy. "Have a seat. I'll be right back."

After a quick dash to the kitchen, she returned with a tray of food and two frosty glasses of fresh strawberry lemonade. "I hope this is okay. I thought since we had things to discuss, I'd just whip something up for us instead of having you order off the menu."

Ryan blinked and then his mouth curved into an actual smile. Amanda almost wished she'd tucked her phone into the pocket of her jeans so she could take a picture of it. "Are those what I think they are?"

"Fried green tomatoes?" She nodded. "Yes, but I've done kind of a gourmet spin on them and incorporated them into a caprese salad."

"Wow. Impressive. Is this going to be a new menu addition?"

She wished. Her mom would never go for it. "No, but I like to experiment. Someday I'm hoping to expand the Grille into high-end catering."

She swallowed. Had she just said that out loud?

Other than Belle, she hadn't told a soul about why she'd been playing around with new recipes and posting them to Instagram. Not even her family. Catering from the Main Street Grille was more of a wish than an actual business plan at this point, and now she'd gone and shared it with the editor of *The Spring Forest Chronicle*. "I don't know why I told you that. Please don't put it in the paper."

The corners of his mouth turned up. There was that smile again. "Your secret is safe with me."

She almost wished he'd go back to his normal solemn expression. He was too handsome when he smiled, too charming. It was unnerving. Who knew what that smile would make her say next?

Amanda took a gulp of lemonade as he opened a small notepad.

"The Whitaker sisters spoke very highly of you," he said. "Tell me about your plans for the barbecue fundraiser."

"Birdie and Bunny are sweethearts. I've been volunteering at Furever Paws for about three years now, walking dogs mostly. The Grille is slowest Mondays, so that's my usual day. When I saw how hard the tornado hit the shelter, I wanted to do something to help."

She went on to describe her vision for the cook-off, from the barbecue contest to the games and raffles to her plans for a silent auction and live music. Between bites of food, Ryan took notes. Just as she'd told Belle, it was all very businesslike—a normal interview.

Which was a relief, frankly.

Then, just as they were wrapping things up, Ryan's cell phone buzzed, vibrating across the Formica table. He glanced at it and frowned. "I'm sorry, I should probably take this. It's my son's school."

"Of course." Amanda nodded.

"Hello?" A line etched between his brows, and she knew she should get up and leave, but she couldn't seem to make herself budge. "Yes, this is Dillon's father."

His frown deepened.

She definitely shouldn't still be sitting there, watching him listen to what was obviously a difficult call.

"I, um…" she whispered, sliding toward the edge of the vinyl seat.

But then something wholly unexpected happened. He looked up, shook his head slightly and reached for her hand, covering it with his.

Stay.

He didn't say it. He didn't have to. She could see it in his eyes, could feel it in the desperate touch of his fingertips—a hand that was reaching for something. Reaching for help.

She went still as stone. Unable to move, unable to breathe, staring at his hand on top of hers as she tried her best not to listen to his end of the conversation, catching only snippets—words like *anxiety, grief* and *silence.*

When he ended the call, he sat quietly for a minute, staring down at his phone. Then his gaze slid slowly toward their hands and he blinked, snatching his away. "Sorry. I…"

Heart pounding hard, Amanda buried her hands in her lap under the table. "Don't apologize. It's okay."

"Really, I'm sorry. Dillon didn't want to go outside for recess today. He's having some trouble at school, and I…" he shook his head "…I'm kind of at my wits' end. I thought moving here would be good for him, but I'm beginning to wonder."

A lump formed in her throat. She swallowed around it and took a deep breath. "I've lived here my whole life. It's a nice place. I'm sure he'll come around. Maybe he just needs some time and a little help coming out of his shell."

Ryan lifted weary eyes to hers. "That might be the understatement of the century."

She blurted out the first thing that popped into her head. "Have you thought about bringing him by Furever Paws?"

He shook his head again, with more force this time. "No. Our household is in enough turmoil as it is without adding a pet to the mix. I don't even think I could handle a goldfish at this point."

She let out a laugh before she could stop it. "No pressure. You don't have to take an animal home, but maybe hanging out with some of the dogs and cats will help him feel more at ease. You never know. Petting a dog has been scientifically proved to reduce stress and anxiety."

"You make a strong argument." Ryan nodded slowly. "As well as a mean fried green tomato."

"Thanks." She glanced down at his empty plate.

"Maybe I'll bring Dillon by the shelter. You said you're usually there on Mondays?"

"Yes."

"Okay, then. It's a..." His voice drifted off and he seemed to catch himself before he said more.

But the words floated between them all the same.

It's a date.

Chapter Five

This is a mistake.

Ryan shifted his SUV into Park in the gravel lot of Furever Paws and glanced at Dillon's reflection in the rearview mirror. His son sat perched on his booster seat with the same withdrawn expression he'd been wearing for the past few days.

Ryan sighed. He hadn't been naive enough to expect Dillon to break into a happy dance the minute they pulled into the driveway, but he'd hoped for at least a smile. Or some glimmer of excitement. Anything, really.

No such luck.

He'd been so sure Dillon was on the brink of a breakthrough after their barbecue dinner from the Grille. But then the school had called again with another troublesome report. Not only was Dillon still refusing to speak, but he'd also regularly started staying inside during recess, choosing to sit at his desk instead of joining his classmates outside on the playground.

Ryan was at his breaking point, which was the only explanation for the way he'd behaved at the end of his interview with Amanda Sylvester. If he'd been thinking clearly—if he'd been acting like the professional he used to be—he never would have held her hand during the phone call. He definitely hadn't done anything like that in his previous life. Ever.

There was something about her, though...something beyond physical attraction. Yes, she was beautiful—so beautiful that he'd lain awake at night thinking about the sultry warmth in her eyes and the elegance of her movements. She had a way of making even the simplest tasks seem graceful, whether she was peeling an apple or dusting a pie with powdered sugar. And she had just enough of a Southern accent to make her words fall from her lips soft and smooth, like melted butter.

But beyond those things, for reasons he couldn't begin to understand, he felt like he could talk to her.

That was a first. One of Maggie's biggest complaints during their marriage had been his aloofness. She'd called him noncommunicative so many times he'd lost count, which made his current predicament with Dillon all the more ironic.

He's your *son.* You *did this.*

He pulled the keys from the ignition and forced a smile. "Hey, buddy. We're here. Are you ready to pet some dogs?"

Dillon's gaze found his in the reflection of the rear-view mirror. The boy gave him a barely perceptible nod.

"Great!" Ryan's voice rang with false cheer. He wondered how much longer he could keep up the cheerleader act, how many more weeks or months he had in him.

As long as it takes.

Dillon sat completely still while Ryan unbuckled the booster seat and lifted him out of the car. Hand in hand, they walked toward the shelter building, which looked every bit as worse for wear as it had the day he'd come to interview the Whitaker sisters. Amanda's barbecue fundraiser couldn't come soon enough, apparently. Luckily, it was happening next week.

As if his thoughts had somehow conjured her into being, Amanda waved at him from beyond the chain-link fence surrounding the building. "Hi, Ryan. Hey there, Dillon."

She was dressed in a ruffled gingham top paired with white jeans, and a cheery red leash stretched from her graceful hand to a tiny brown dog lying on his belly at her feet. Ryan waved back, and did his best to ignore the warmth that blossomed in his chest when he realized she'd remembered Dillon's name.

"I'll meet you in the lobby." She pointed to the building. "You'll need to check in at the information desk, and then I'll show you around as soon as I put Tucker here back in his kennel."

Ryan glanced at the dog at the end of the leash— Tucker, presumably. Amanda gave the leash a tug, and the pup didn't budge. Probably because it looked exactly like the kind of animal that got toted around in a handbag instead of walking on its own four legs.

He glanced back up at Amanda just in time to see her cheeks flare pink before she scooped the dog into her arms and carried him out of sight. Again, he felt a strange pull toward her—the same pull that had caused him to reach for her hand during their phone call the other day—and he wondered what on earth he was doing here. The last thing he needed in his life was a pet.

But he was here now, and despite Ryan's many reminders that they wouldn't be going home with a new dog or a cat, Dillon was suddenly looking somewhat interested. His gaze trailed after Amanda, then he peered up at Ryan as the corner of his mouth tugged into a grin.

Ryan gave his hand a squeeze. "Come on, bud. Let's go."

The shelter lobby looked about the same as it had the last time he'd seen it. Water still dripped from the ceiling in a handful of places, and the room smelled like a wet paper bag. Not exactly a good sign. Ryan was somewhat surprised they hadn't managed to even start on the badly needed repairs, but maybe Birdie and Bunny were waiting to see how much money the barbecue fundraiser pulled in. Still, they needed to get a jump on things. Surely most of the mess would be covered by their insurance policy.

"Welcome to Furever Paws." An elderly man sitting at the front desk smiled as they walked in. A tiny orange kitten sat nestled in his lap.

Dillon sneaked a glance at the cat from behind Ryan's leg.

The shelter volunteer winked at Ryan, then craned his neck to catch Dillon's attention. "Would you like to pet Lucille, son? She's a real sweetheart."

"Go ahead. It's okay. That's why we're here." Ryan let go of Dillon's hand and gave him an encouraging nudge between his tiny shoulder blades.

By some miracle, it worked. Dillon took a few tentative steps forward until the kitten was within reach, and then he ran his fingertips gently over the animal's tiny orange head.

"I think she likes you," Ryan said.

A soft, rumbling purr came from the little kitten, and Dillon smiled a smile that Ryan hadn't seen for weeks. Maybe even months.

"You're a genius," Ryan whispered as Amanda slipped into the lobby and came to stand quietly beside him. "Thank you."

She shrugged one shoulder. "I'm hardly a genius. What kid doesn't love baby animals?"

She didn't get it. How could she?

"No, seriously." Ryan swallowed. He was jaded enough not to let himself hope this was some kind of breakthrough, but he'd take a joyous moment when he could get it. This was one of them. *"Thank you."*

Amanda blinked up at him, and a flicker of understanding passed through her gaze—just enough of one to make him wonder if maybe she *did* get it, after all. "I'm happy to help."

A silence settled over them, so tender and sweet that

Ryan had to look away before he did something crazy again, like hold her hand.

Or possibly something even crazier, like kiss her.

He cleared his throat. "I should probably go sign us in."

"Not necessary." Amanda grinned at the man behind the desk. "Hans, Ryan and Dillon are with me."

"Yes, ma'am." Hans winked at Dillon. "You have fun now, son. Miss Lucille will be right here with me if you decide to adopt her."

"We're just here to look and spend some time with the animals," Ryan said automatically, because that's what he'd been telling himself ever since Amanda had suggested Dillon might like to visit the shelter.

But seeing the sudden sag in Dillon's tiny shoulders gave him pause. Maybe a cat wouldn't be so bad. They mostly took care of themselves, didn't they?

"No pressure. I promise." Amanda bent to look Dillon in the eyes. "Are you ready to go meet some of the other pets?"

He nodded again, and then he slipped his hand into Amanda's as if he'd known her his entire life.

The warmth in Ryan's chest deepened into a cavernous ache that felt all too much like attraction. Want. *Need.*

He couldn't have her. No way, no how. He'd come to Spring Forest to concentrate on fatherhood and nothing else. He had neither the time nor the energy for a relationship. Sharing a meal with Amanda Sylvester was mostly safe. Holding hands with her was borderline.

But watching Amanda interact with his troubled son was definitely more than he could take.

Why did he suddenly have the feeling that adopting a pet might be just the least of his worries?

"Before we head to the dog kennel, I thought you might like to see the farm animals." Amanda led Dillon through the shelter building while Ryan trailed behind and kept a protective hand on his son's back.

The little boy hadn't uttered a single word since they'd arrived. Come to think of it, she couldn't remember if he'd said anything the other night when they'd come to pick up their barbecue dinners at the Grille, either. The poor kid was so shy, and something about his big warm eyes and the sweet dimple in his chin tugged at her heartstrings in a major way.

Maybe because he looks exactly like his father.

She sneaked a quick glance at Ryan as they exited the building and stepped into the dazzling sunshine. Those honey-colored eyes of his were nothing short of captivating. She forced herself to look away.

This wasn't a date. Absolutely not. She was simply being neighborly. As lovely as Ryan Carter's eyes were, there was a weariness to them she hadn't noticed until he'd thanked her for encouraging him to bring Dillon to the shelter. Whatever troubles Dillon was having at school were clearly just the tip of the iceberg.

She wondered what had happened back in Washington, DC. The Spring Forest rumor mill was rife with speculation—so much so that Amanda had broken down and googled Ryan. Apparently, he'd been a big-time editor at *The Washington Post*. She'd even stumbled upon a photograph of him at the White House, standing beside the president. But then her gaze had snagged on someone else in the picture—a beautiful woman with her arm linked through Ryan's—and she'd slammed her laptop closed.

"We've got pigs, sheep, goats and even a couple llamas." Amanda pointed past Birdie and Bunny's rambling Victorian farmhouse and the garden gate, toward the paddock.

When Dillon rose up on tiptoes to catch a glimpse, Ryan scooped him up and swung him onto his shoulders. Adorable. Amanda's heart gave a rebellious little flutter.

She was about to launch into tour guide mode to distract herself from their precious father-and-son vibe when one of the llamas charged the fence and began to prance back and forth.

Amanda slowed to a stop. "That's weird. I've never seen Llama Bean behave that way before."

Ryan made a strange coughing noise and when she glanced at him, he grimaced. "I have."

"Seriously? When?"

"When I came out to interview the Whitaker sisters." His face turned a fascinating shade of red. "Birdie seems to think Llama Bean has a crush on me."

"That's…interesting." Laughter bubbled up Amanda's throat. Not that she couldn't relate the tiniest bit to Llama Bean all of a sudden. "And also hilarious."

"Tell me I'm not the only one and we're just dealing with a boy-crazy llama." Ryan shot her a hopeful glance.

"Afraid not." She laughed again, harder this time. "Only you."

Even Dillon looked like he was on the verge of letting out a giggle.

Amanda shaded her eyes with her hand and peered up at him. "What do you think? Should we take pity on your dad and skip the paddock? I have a few dogs who are anxious to meet you."

He nodded, eyes shining bright, and Amanda could suddenly feel her pulse pounding in her throat.

Don't get attached.

Of course she wouldn't. She could barely manage the additional responsibility of new houseplants. She had no business taking on a single dad and his wounded son. Besides, she was pretty certain Ryan didn't need her help. As she was all too aware, he was a fully grown man.

"Off to the kennels, then." Amanda waved at one very disappointed llama as they all headed back to the shelter building.

One by one, they visited the dogs in the kennels. The pups greeted Dillon with a frenzy of yips and wagging tails. He seemed to take a shine to Charlie, a one-year-old yellow Lab pup. Amanda brought the dog out of his kennel so Dillon could pet him.

"I think Charlie likes you almost as much as Llama Bean likes your dad." Amanda stifled a grin as the Lab squirmed with excitement at Dillon's feet.

"I think you might be right." Ryan laughed.

The big dog's tail beat against the little boy's shins and he took a backward step.

"Labs are pretty boisterous at this age," Amanda said.

As if on cue, Charlie hopped to his feet and swiped Dillon's face with a sloppy, wet lick of his big pink tongue. Dillon pulled a face.

Ryan's gaze slid toward Amanda. "I'm getting the feeling that he might be more of a cat person."

Amanda nodded. "Note taken. Hey Dillon, why don't we pop over to the cat room? It's right next door."

His dark curls bobbed as he nodded his head, and she melted a little bit. He really was the most darling child.

Once Charlie was placed safely back inside his kennel, she led their trio toward the cat room. The dog kennel area had started to fill up with potential adopters, which was a great thing, obviously. But somehow Dillon seemed to get lost in the shuffle, because once Amanda and Ryan reached the door, he was no longer nestled between them as he'd been for the majority of the visit.

"Dillon?" Ryan's head swiveled back and forth, sweeping the area. The hint of alarm in his voice made Amanda's stomach tumble.

"He was right here a second ago. I'm sure he's close by." She reached for Ryan as naturally as if touching him was something she'd done a million times, resting her fingertips lightly on his forearm. A zing of electricity shot through her and she snatched her hand back. "Um…"

Their eyes met and held, but then Ryan's gaze drifted over her head. "There he is!"

She spun around and sure enough, Dillon stood behind them, less than three feet away. He was facing one of the kennels, staring intently at the dog inside—Tucker.

"Oh." Amanda blinked.

Well, this is an interesting development.

Ryan crouched down beside Dillon and wrapped an arm around his shoulders. "Hey bud, you scared me. I was worried I'd lost you for a second. I thought you wanted to go see the cats."

The child shook his head and pointed at Tucker sitting quietly in the back corner of his kennel. As usual, he was the only dog in the building who refused to come forward and greet visitors.

Ryan shot a questioning glance at Amanda.

"This is Tucker. He's a little…" *aloof, cranky, irritable* "…bashful."

If dogs could roll their eyes, Tucker would have done so right then and there.

Dillon, however, remained glued to the spot as if he'd just spotted his new best friend.

So she relented. "But if you want to pet him, we can give it a try."

She cast a pleading glance at the dog as she unfastened the lock on the kennel door. *Be nice.* By some miracle, it worked, because instead of having to bribe him with a cheese cube to walk out of the enclosure, he trotted toward them with an unprecedented spring in his step.

"Tucker is a chiweenie—half Chihuahua, half dachshund." She gathered the dog into her arms and held him while Dillon gave him a tentative pat on the head.

Tucker was notoriously averse to being touched anywhere other than his back. He usually tried to squirm out of reach, but before she could instruct Dillon on how to pet the picky dog, Tucker closed his eyes and burrowed into his touch.

What was happening?

"Wow, he normally doesn't like that at all." It was a fluke. It had to be.

But the more Dillon petted the cantankerous dog, the sweeter Tucker became. He was practically morphing into a marshmallow in her arms.

"Why don't we go to one of the adoption rooms so you two can spend some quality time together?" She glanced up Ryan. "Don't worry. I'm not trying to force this dog on you or anything, but a cozy place to visit will be nice, don't you think?"

He nodded without tearing his gaze away from Dillon's glowing face.

The shelter only had two visitation rooms—one for cats and the other for dogs—and luckily, both were free. As Amanda carried Tucker inside, she whispered into his furry ear, "Whatever has come over you, keep it up. This little boy needs a friend."

His only response was a twitch of his ear, but when Dillon plopped down cross-legged on the floor, the pup scurried over to him.

"Look at those little legs go," Ryan said. "I'm guessing he's a lapdog."

"Today he is." Amanda shook her head. "I can't tell you how unusual this is, though. Tucker is normally pretty standoffish. He's been adopted out twice, but neither time worked out. He just never seems to bond with anyone."

Ryan shot her a look as Tucker climbed into Dillon's lap and curled into a contented ball of fluff.

"He sure seems to like Dillon, though." She grinned.

Ryan arched a brow. "Why do I have the feeling I'm toast?"

"Are you absolutely sure you don't want to adopt a dog?" Amanda murmured.

Ryan's mouth curved into a tender smile. He was indeed toast. Tucker might as well as pack his bags. But before Ryan could give her an answer, a winsome, childlike voice broke through the loaded silence.

"Please, Daddy."

Chapter Six

Ryan's hands shook so badly that he could barely fill out the Furever Paws adoption application. He was a mess—a stunned, jittery, happy as hell mess.

At last, Dillon had spoken. He couldn't believe it. He hadn't heard his son's voice in nearly a year, and the sound was so sweet, so damned wonderful that he'd nearly fallen to his knees and wept like a baby.

How long had he hoped and prayed for something like this? Weeks...*months*...and when it finally happened, he'd been so shaken he could only choke out a response.

Yes.

Yes, of course they'd take the dog home. Ryan didn't have a choice, did he? It was the ultimate reward for the most precious two words he'd ever heard. He'd have adopted every animal in the building if that's what Dillon had asked him to do.

"Are you okay?" Amanda sat down beside him at the adoption counselor's desk. The volunteer counselor had moved on to help another potential pet parent since Amanda and the Whitaker sisters had personally vouched for Ryan and Dillon, but there was still a fair amount of paperwork to contend with. "You seem rattled."

"I am rattled." His throat clogged, and he swallowed hard. God, was he actually going to cry in front of Amanda Sylvester? *Get it together.*

"Is there anything I can do to help? Birdie and Bunny are keeping an eye on Dillon right now. They're positively thrilled that you two are taking Tucker home." She bit her lip, and for a second Ryan forgot he was in the throes of an emotional turning point and fixated on her mouth. So pretty, so pink.

So undeniably kissable.

He raked a trembling hand through his hair and let out a measured breath.

"Unless you've had second thoughts about adopting a dog?" She frowned. "I know that wasn't your intention when you agreed to stop by."

"No second thoughts at all. I've actually never been so sure about anything in my life. When Dillon spoke just now…" Ryan stared down at the papers in front of him until the letters on the page blended into a teary blur.

Then he pressed the heels of his hands against his eyes before meeting Amanda's concerned gaze head-on.

"Sorry, I need to explain. I told you about the difficulties Dillon has been having at school, but you don't know the extent of it. Dillon hasn't talked since his mother died last year."

Amanda's fingertips fluttered to her throat. "At all?"

"Not a word." He took another deep breath. "Not until you introduced him to that silly little dog."

"Oh my God, this is huge."

He nodded. "Indeed it is. I don't know the first thing about dogs. I've never owned one before—not even as a kid. But yeah, I'm absolutely filling out these adoption papers. I'll just have to figure out being a dog owner as we go along."

"I'm so happy for you." Amanda's eyes glittered, and the urge to kiss her was almost overwhelming.

For the first time in practically as long as he could remember, Ryan felt like someone was on his side. Even before Maggie had died, he'd always felt more alone than part of a team. Their marriage had been tumultuous from the start, which probably had a lot to do with why he'd become such a workaholic.

But the look in Amanda's eyes reminded him what it was like to be connected to another person, to know someone genuinely *cared*. Ryan hadn't realized quite how much he'd missed feeling that way until now.

"Tucker and Dillon were made for each other," she continued. "I think it's meant to be. It kind of makes you believe in fate, doesn't it?"

Fate.

Is that what this was? Ryan didn't know, and he was afraid to examine it too closely. Because if fate led Dillon to Tucker, he might be tempted to believe it had also set Amanda squarely into his own path. And he couldn't go there. Today had been a good day—his first good day in a long, lonely time—but his life was still a train wreck. It would be wrong to drag someone else into his mess, especially someone as lovely as Amanda Sylvester.

Yet he couldn't seem to stop himself from asking her a question that would ensure her continued presence in his and Dillon's chaotic life. "I don't suppose you'd be willing to help us get settled into a routine with the dog? You seem to know a lot about Tucker."

"I do." She grinned. "And I'd love to help. If you're a first-time dog owner, you could probably use some assistance."

Wasn't that what dog training books were for? Not to mention pet supply stores, online communities and obedience classes. There was an entire industry out there devoted to pet care, but for some unknown reason, he felt compelled to ask Amanda to help him instead.

Or maybe the reason was obvious, but he wasn't ready to accept it. "Great, thanks. I probably shouldn't ask. You've already done so much…"

"Don't mention it. I'm happy to give you a few pointers. I want the adjustment to go as smoothly as possible. Tucker's a special little guy. Dillon too, obviously." The gleam in her soft brown eyes turned mischievous. "According to Llama Bean, so are you."

"It's nice to know the llama put in a good word for me," he said dryly.

A week ago, he would probably have insisted Llama Bean was the only living soul who believed in him, but he was beginning to think that might not be the case after all.

Amanda paused on Ryan's doorstep the next morning, hesitant to ring the bell.

She'd accompanied him and Dillon to the pet store the previous afternoon, ensuring they purchased all the necessary items to welcome a new dog into their home. They'd piled the shopping cart high with chew toys, food and water bowls, kibble, dog shampoo, a training crate, treats and a shiny red leash with a matching collar. Then she'd told Ryan everything he needed to know in order to survive their first night with Tucker, including the basics of crate training. She'd even helped Dillon use the engraving machine at the pet store to make a personalized tag for Tucker with his name and their address.

Anyone observing their interaction probably would have thought that Amanda was part of the family. A few times, she might have even felt that way herself—like when Dillon wanted her to choose Tucker's dog bed or when Ryan insisted they ride together to the pet store. She'd sunk into the warm comfort of the passenger seat of his new SUV while Dillon smiled at her from his booster chair in the back seat.

Still, as cozy at it had been at times, she knew better than to believe it meant anything. Ryan had asked for her help with Tucker, and of course she'd agreed. She loved that dog and wanted to see him happy in his permanent home. And since Ryan was an inexperienced dog owner, he'd definitely need all the help he could get—especially with a stubborn dog like Tucker. She was basically only here as an amateur dog trainer.

But of course she'd woken up at four in the morning, anxious about the day ahead. Her mind knew there was nothing to be nervous about, but her body hadn't quite gotten the memo. So after an hour of staring at the ceiling, she'd gotten up and made breakfast. Nothing special—French baked toast with cream and eggs. And now here she was, standing on the front porch of Ryan's modest home in the historic Kingdom Creek neighborhood of Spring Forest, casserole dish in hand.

She took a deep breath and rang the bell, somehow suppressing the urge to dump the baking dish behind the nearest bush. She was a cook, after all, so it wasn't weird that she'd brought breakfast along to their first in-home dog training session.

Was it?

Too late now. You're holding a classic French country meal in your best Le Creuset.

The door swung open, revealing yet another version of Ryan Carter she'd never seen before. This one wore running shorts paired with a gray Georgetown University T-shirt and a charmingly rumpled case of bedhead. He held a smug-looking Tucker in one hand and a chewed up running shoe in the other. Of all the versions of Ryan, it was by far Amanda's favorite— so sweetly masculine that she nearly dropped her casserole.

"Good morning." She flashed him a wobbly smile.

"Morning." Ryan's gaze dropped to the dish in her hands as Tucker's tail beat against his side. "What is that amazing smell?"

"Oeufs au plat bressane." When his expression went blank, she added, "French toast and eggs with cream."

He tilted his head, and a sleepy smile came to his lips—one that made her imagine him in bed, tangled in sheets and nothing else. "You made us breakfast?"

"Um." Definitely awkward. God, she wanted to die. "I couldn't sleep, and the kitchen is just kind of my happy place. You don't have to eat it."

"Are you kidding? Try to stop me." He opened the door wider. "Please come in."

The door clicked closed behind her, and she followed him toward a cozy kitchen with a big bay window overlooking a backyard with an old-fashioned tire swing. It was her favorite sort of kitchen, warm and inviting. She could easily imagine whipping up after-school snacks for Dillon in a space like this one. Or Christmas cookies during the holidays—tiny gingerbread versions of herself, Ryan and Dillon.

She nibbled on her bottom lip. Fantasizing about family life with Ryan and his son wasn't going to get her any closer to her dream of expanding into catering. "How did things go last night with Tucker?"

"Great," he said a little too brightly.

Amanda set the casserole dish down on the butcher block island in the center of the room and waited for Ryan to meet her gaze. Once he did, she cast a pointed glance at the destroyed Nike in his grip. "The shoe in your hand says otherwise."

"Busted." He dropped the sneaker and held Tucker toward her. "Maybe you should hold this monster while I set the table so he doesn't get into any more trouble."

"Gladly." She gathered the little chiweenie in her arms, just as she'd done a thousand times before, and pressed a kiss to the top of his furry head.

Tucker didn't flinch like he normally did when she showered him with unwanted affection. He smelled different too—less like the institutional soap Birdie and Bunny used to clean the shelter and more like something she couldn't quite put her finger on. But it reminded her of sunny summer picnics and running through the sprinkler on fresh-cut grass...of childhood.

"I'm sorry about the shoe," she said. "I hope you're not having second thoughts about keeping Tucker."

"Absolutely not." Ryan's T-shirt pulled tight against his muscular back as he opened a cabinet and reached inside for a stack of plates.

Amanda tried not to stare, but failed miserably, prompting Tucker to let out a knowing snort. The little guy might belong to Ryan and Dillon now, but he still seemed to be able to read Amanda's mind. Some things never changed.

Ryan arranged the plates on a cozy table tucked beside the window, then turned to face her.

"Dillon is like a completely different kid. He's still not saying much, but that's okay. There's a light in his eyes that I haven't seen in a really long time, and last night when I tucked him into bed, he thanked me for letting him bring Tucker home with us." He inhaled a ragged breath. "He thanked me out loud, with his voice. Honestly, I nearly lost it right then and there."

Amanda tightened her hold on Tucker lest she reach out to give Ryan a hug. "That's amazing. It sounds like all three of you just might have found a happy ending."

"I'm not sure I'd go that far yet. We've still got a long road ahead of us, but for the first time in a while, I can actually see a glimmer of light at the end of the tunnel." He gave Tucker a scratch behind his ears. "This little guy could chew up every pair of shoes I own and I'd still let him stay."

"I don't think that'll be necessary. Some supervision and a good-sized rawhide chew should solve that problem." She gave Ryan a wry smile. Or at least she tried, but he was suddenly closer to her than he'd ever been before. *Too* close.

He was so beautiful that it hurt to look at him at such close range. She felt a bittersweet pang in her heart, and reminded herself that the only reason he was standing mere inches away was so that he could pet Tucker. But then his fingertips grew still on the dog's tiny head and he lifted his gaze to hers, and she could barely breathe.

"Why are you doing this?" His voice was as deep and delicious as devil's food cake.

Her head spun a little, like it sometimes did when she ate too much sugar. "Doing what?"

"Everything—taking us to the shelter, helping out with Tucker's training." The corner of his mouth hitched up, drawing every ounce of her attention to his mouth. "Cooking us breakfast."

That stupid, stupid French casserole. *Quel* embarrassment. "I couldn't sleep, remember? It's nothing."

"It isn't nothing. It's *something*." His hand moved to her cheek, cupping it in a way that made her want to lean into him and close her eyes. "A very special something...something that makes it impossible for me to ignore how very much I want to kiss you."

Seriously?

The secret key to being kissed by Ryan Carter was a dish of eggs, bread and cream? If she'd known that, she would have drowned the man in breakfast offerings weeks ago.

"You want to kiss me?" she breathed.

The pad of his thumb grazed her bottom lip. "Very much. Sometimes it's all I can think about."

Suddenly, it was all she could think about too. That, and running her fingers through his elegantly rumpled hair. If she hadn't still been clutching Tucker, she probably would have done it.

Happiness sparkled inside her, making her brave. Bold. "Why haven't you, then?"

"For a lot of reasons." He swallowed, and his eyes glittered. "But right now I can't seem to remember any of them. So can I..."

"Yes," she said without waiting for him to respond. "Please, please kiss me."

Then, before she could process what was happening—before her nerves had a chance to take over and ruin everything—his mouth came down on hers, warm and wanting. And in that cozy kitchen, with Tucker nestled softly between them, Amanda's secret crush became not-so-secret anymore. Because to her complete and utter astonishment, she was kissing Ryan Carter.

Ryan's first thought when his lips brushed against Amanda's was that she tasted even sweeter than he'd imagined. Lush and exquisite, like brandy-soaked cherries and soft velvet mornings. His arousal was instantaneous, as if he'd never kissed a woman before in his life. Probably because he hadn't. Not in this life, anyway—the new one he'd worked so hard to create for himself and Dillon after Maggie had died.

Sometimes he felt like he'd ceased to exist since that terrible day. The shock of losing her had been devastating, even though his marriage had been hanging on by a thread. Her death had somehow frozen him in time, suspended in a dreadful tangle of guilt and regret. According to the police report, she'd just left an attorney's office on the afternoon of her accident. Ryan wasn't sure why she'd been there, and he'd never asked. He doubted the lawyer would tell him, even if he had tried to find out. Besides, what difference did it make now?

In his heart, though, he knew.

The only reason she would have left Dillon at home with a sitter was that she'd been inquiring about a divorce. Which meant the blame for her death rested at least partially on his weary shoulders. He tried not to think about it, especially once Dillon disappeared into his quiet, lonely world, but the truth was always there, lurking beneath the surface.

Not now, though. The touch of Amanda's lips drew him gently and fully into the present. He felt complete again. Whole. No longer just a husk of the man he'd once been, but someone different and new. Someone who might not be destined to repeat the mistakes of his past. His previous life seemed far away—just a blip in his memory—and the hidden corner of his soul ordinarily reserved for remorse glimmered with something shiny and new.

Hope.

Amanda's lips parted even more, and his tongue slid against hers. Slowly…reverently. Then she made a little whimpering sound, as delicate as a kitten, and he scooped the dog out of her arms and set him on the floor.

Let Tucker tear the house down. Ryan didn't give a damn. For once, he wanted to stop worrying, stop thinking, stop trying to micromanage every second of his existence, as if he had any control over his life whatsoever. He just wanted to taste and feel and ache.

So he did. He ached so much that when Amanda lifted her arms and wrapped them around his neck, he groaned and deepened their kiss as if she held the key to happiness somewhere in her glorious valentine of a mouth. Hell, maybe she did.

All night he'd been wondering about Dillon and the dog, trying to understand their connection. He kept turning it over in his mind, but his thoughts kept leading him back to the same place—her. Amanda.

She'd been there the night of the barbecue dinner, the best night he'd had with Dillon since moving to Spring Forest. She'd been there, holding his hand, when he'd gotten the most recent phone call from Dillon's school. And she'd been there again when Dillon stumbled upon Tucker and Furever Paws. Somewhere deep down, Ryan was beginning to abandon the theory that it was all coincidence. There was something undeniably special about Amanda Sylvester.

"You," he whispered, resting his forehead against hers and sliding his hands into her hair. It was the only syllable he could force out of his mouth when he wanted to say so much more. He wanted to ask her things, to dig for answers because the journalist in him couldn't shake the need to know.

Who are you?

What are you doing to me...to us?

Is any of this real, or will it all slip away soon?

Her gaze bore into his, heated and drowsy with desire. What were they doing? Dillon was right down the hall, getting dressed for school. What would Ryan say if he walked into the kitchen and found him kissing a woman who wasn't his mother? He'd waited a long time for his son to start talking again. He couldn't risk ruining things now.

The beatific smile on Amanda's face faded ever so slightly, as if she knew he'd started thinking again instead of letting his heart lead the way. Or worse—as if she thought they'd just made a terrible mistake.

But they hadn't.

Had they?

"Um..." She raised a hand to her lips, touching them where his mouth had been just moments ago. "I shouldn't have asked you to do that."

Please, please kiss me.

Her words hung in the space between them. Ryan could still hear them, crystal clear, as if they'd been absorbed into the walls where they could haunt him day and night. Every time he closed his eyes.

"I'm sorry." She took a backward step, just out of reach.

Ryan held out his hands anyway. He grasped at air and opened his mouth to tell her, *No. Don't be sorry. Don't* ever *be sorry.* But before he could say a thing, the iPhone sitting on the kitchen counter blared to life. His ringtone—the theme song to Dillon's favorite cartoon—was in such jarring opposition to the private silence that had enveloped them just moments before that Ryan blinked, and wondered for a second if maybe he'd imagined the entire encounter.

But Amanda was right there, almost close enough to touch, with kiss-swollen lips and eyes that sparkled with intimacy. He wasn't dreaming. She was real. *The kiss* had been real, and it had been the best damned kiss of his life.

The phone rang again, and she glanced at it. "Do you need to get that?"

"It can wait," he said without checking the caller ID.

Why bother? Everyone in the world he cared most about was safe beneath this very roof. This wasn't like the call he'd gotten a year ago…the one that had changed everything. Besides, he needed to make sure she knew he didn't regret what had just happened.

But mere seconds after the ringing stopped, it started up again. This time, they both swiveled their heads in the direction of his phone, vibrating on the counter.

Finally, he looked down at the screen and took in the caller ID. "It's my in-laws." Of course. Ryan sighed and tried to tamp down the quick flare of panic spreading in his chest. He'd done nothing wrong. For crying out loud, he wasn't even married anymore. He was free to kiss whomever he wanted. "My former in-laws, I mean."

Amanda nodded, but didn't seem convinced. Meanwhile, the phone kept blaring that awful sound.

"I'm sure it's about Dillon. They tend to call and check on him a lot." His jaw tightened. "If I don't answer it, they're going to keep at it."

Or they might do what they'd done the last time he'd ignored their call. The night of the barbecue dinner, Annabelle had left a worried message on his voice mail and when he hadn't immediately responded, she'd then followed it up with emails to both his personal and business accounts and several calls to the paper. Ryan couldn't have them ringing *The Spring Forest Chronicle* and interrogating Jonah.

"Just wait." He touched her wrist, wrapping his fingers loosely around it like a bracelet while he grabbed the phone with his other hand. *"Please."*

"Take the call. It's fine, I promise." She nodded toward Tucker, trotting past them with the remains of Ryan's running shoe dangling from his mouth. "I'll make sure your dog is entertained."

He nodded, released her wrist with no small amount

of reluctance and pressed Accept on his phone's small screen. "Hello?"

"There you are. We were beginning to worry." Maggie's mother huffed out a sigh.

"Dillon's just fine, Annabelle. We both are." Ryan stopped short of telling her it was good to hear from her, because he didn't see the point in lying. Also, he didn't want to encourage the daily interrogation.

Not that it would help. He'd moved six hours away in an effort to put a stop to their hovering, but Annabelle and Finch still hadn't gotten the point.

"I called the other day and never heard anything back," she said.

Not true. He'd returned her email, but now wasn't the occasion to argue. "We've been busy. And actually, Dillon needs to be at school in less than an hour, so can we give you a call back this evening?"

Annabelle sniffed. "That won't be necessary." Relief flitted through Ryan for the briefest of moments, but before he could say anything else, she dropped a bomb into the middle of the conversation. "Finch and I are coming to visit."

He sank into one of the kitchen chairs. "Annabelle, please."

It wasn't the right time. Dillon was just beginning to get settled. He needed a few more weeks. Was that really so much to expect?

"Surely you don't expect us to ask permission to see our only grandchild." She waited a beat, but not long enough for him to formulate any kind of reasonable response. "The lack of communication has been frustrating. We still can't get a word out of Dillon, so we have no way of knowing what kind of environment he's being raised in."

His gaze cut to Amanda. He should have let the call roll to voice mail again. This definitely wasn't the type of conversation he should be having in front of her mere moments after they'd had their first kiss.

Who was he kidding? It would probably be their *only* kiss.

She scooped Tucker into her arms and carried him out of the room.

Ryan lowered his voice. "That's not fair, Annabelle. Dillon is happy here. He has a brand-new dog, and he's started speaking again."

"Excellent. Put him on the phone."

And have her pressure Dillon into talking to her? He might clam up all over again. Ryan couldn't— *wouldn't*—take that risk. "The situation is still delicate. Why don't we arrange a time to Skype later this evening after Dillon comes home from school?"

"That would be lovely, but we're still coming. We've already purchased our plane tickets. We'll see you at the end of the month."

The line went dead before he could utter another protest.

Great. The end of the month was only three weeks away, which gave him less than twenty-one days to master both dog training and parenting before his former in-laws did something even more drastic than bombarding him with a surprise visit.

He could do this. Things were already improving, thanks to a scrappy little dog.

And Amanda.

Amanda. Damn it. Where had she gone?

He got up, left his phone behind and darted to the living room. But she wasn't there. She wasn't anywhere he looked, and when he spotted Tucker happily gnawing on a giant bone on his new plaid dog bed, Ryan understood why.

She'd kept her promise to make sure the dog was entertained.

And then she'd left.

Chapter Seven

"So let me get this straight." Belle gave her apron strings a yank and tied them into a firm bow. "You kissed him, and then you ran."

Why, oh why, had Amanda told her about the kiss?

"Shhh." Amanda cast a pointed glance at Roberto, chopping carrots at the other end of the industrial kitchen and once again pretending he couldn't hear what was happening around him. If Amanda ever became famous—or far more likely, *infamous*—that man would probably make a fortune penning her unauthorized tell-all biography.

But for now he didn't appear to care. As far as she could tell, he'd also managed to keep a lid on all of the other embarrassing secrets he'd overheard, so when

Belle rolled her eyes and gave zero indication of abandoning her line of questioning, Amanda relented.

"You know, when I mentioned it last night as we were locking up, I didn't think we'd be revisiting it." She waved her arms around. "Especially here."

"Seriously? You thought you could just slip that into our parting conversation and I wouldn't follow up? It's like you don't know me at all." Belle crossed her arms. "Besides, where else would we discuss it? You're *always* working."

She had a point. "Fine, but you've got it all wrong. I didn't *run*."

She'd simply left without saying goodbye. It would've been weird to stay while Ryan had what was obviously an uncomfortable call with his late wife's parents, wouldn't it? He'd probably only asked her to wait to be polite since she'd made him breakfast like she was auditioning to be the next Betty Crocker. She could help him with Tucker's training later when he wasn't embroiled in family drama…and when she wasn't weak in the knees from the best kiss she'd ever had. So she'd done the only sensible thing—she'd fled.

But she most definitely hadn't run. At worst, she'd speed-walked.

"And *I* didn't kiss *him*. It was the other way around." She added a dash of cardamom to the batter in the silver bowl attached to her KitchenAid mixer. It was her secret ingredient. Why make plain old banana bread when you could make chai-spiced banana bread instead?

Belle pushed her next ingredient out of reach. "You

know you want to talk about it. You always bake when you're freaking out."

Amanda couldn't argue—not when she was surrounded by the evidence of the three pies and the batch of sweet potato biscuits she'd whipped up since 6:00 a.m. "Okay, yes. I'm freaking out. But only a little. And only because it's been three whole days since he kissed me, and I haven't heard a word from him."

She shouldn't have breathed a word about the kiss to Belle, but if she'd kept it bottled up inside for another day, she would have lost her mind. Even baking wasn't helping.

"I repeat: he kissed you and *you ran*. You probably scared the poor guy to death," Belle said.

Amanda's face went warm. "Thanks, that makes me feel loads better. Good talk."

Belle shrugged. "It's a step up from vomiting, I'll give you that."

Roberto let out a snort.

"You're both fired this time." Amanda wagged a finger back and forth between them. "Right after the lunch rush."

"Ignore her, Roberto. This is the tenth time I've been fired this month." Belle cocked her head. "Now that I think about it, every time it's been related somehow to Mr. Hotshot Newspaperman. Someone's crush is getting out of hand."

"It's not a crush," Amanda countered.

It was so much worse than that.

Seeing Ryan at home had reminded her what it had felt like growing up in a home bursting with family, and it made her feel oddly hollow inside. She'd always been too busy at the Grille to even think about marriage or kids. Plus that would have required her to flirt at some point and give dating an actual shot. She hadn't even been able to make room in her life for Tucker, and it had never bothered her much because she had goals. But in reality, she was no closer to branching the restaurant into high-end catering today than she'd been a year ago. Not really.

She was going to be stuck running the same old incarnation of the Main Street Grille for the rest of her life.

Alone.

She could see herself, plain as day, making loaf after loaf of banana bread in the same boring kitchen until she fell over dead. And something about that tire swing in Ryan's backyard, coupled with the way Tucker looked so content in the crook of Ryan's arm, had made her go a little crazy. It made her want things she hadn't thought she'd wanted at all. Otherwise, she never would have asked him to kiss her. Never in a million years.

But she had. And for those few minutes when his hands were in her hair and his mouth moved against hers, she'd forgotten all about the Grille. It could have burned to the ground right then and she wouldn't have noticed. The instant his lips had touched hers, she'd begun to want more. More life. More experiences that made her weak in the knees.

More *everything*.

And it scared her senseless.

"Whatever. I think you should talk to him. Didn't

you promise to help him with Tucker?" Belle shook her head. "That dog is probably running circles around him."

Amanda glared at her. Belle was homing in on her weak spot. Poor Tucker had already been adopted twice, and neither home had worked out. If anything or any-*one* could make her swallow her pride and face Ryan again, it was that squatty little grump of a dog.

"Point taken. I'll drop by Ryan's house and check on Tucker after Dillon gets out of school this afternoon." Maybe if Dillon was nearby, she could manage to look Ryan in the eye without begging him to kiss her again. Then again, that hadn't stopped her before, had it?

"Or you could head over to *The Spring Forest Chronicle* and bring him some coffee. I heard he's been going to Whole Bean, and you know our coffee is better than theirs is." Belle smirked.

She was baiting her, and Amanda knew it. Since the day Whole Bean opened, Amanda insisted the Grille still had the best coffee in town, their notable lack of fancy espresso machines and moody baristas notwithstanding. Ryan deserved better.

And she *had* promised to help with Tucker.

Also, the odds of accidentally kissing him again would be even slimmer in his newsroom.

"I'll think about it, but first I've got to get this banana bread in the oven." And then maybe hide until all her employees forgot she'd kissed Ryan Carter.

"Whatever you say." Belle pushed through the swinging door toward the dining room, then poked her head back in to add, "But just so you know, I heard the Whole Bean uses commercial milk for their lattes instead of the fancy farm-to-table stuff you insist on buying. Ryan is always trying to order those here, so he's probably over there guzzling factory milk at this very moment."

Now she was playing dirty.

Amanda finished mixing her banana bread batter, divided it into three loaf pans and tossed them in the oven, all the while imagining Ryan drinking coffee that had probably been roasted in ten-ton batches somewhere up north, flavored with milk from poor, pitiful cows that lived on a factory farm instead of real Carolina cattle that grazed in the lush green valleys that bordered the Blue Ridge Mountains. Sometimes Amanda even served milk from Birdie and Bunny's sweet dairy cow.

The man clearly had no idea what he was missing.

She untied her apron and threw it on the counter in a lump. "I'll be right back."

Without glancing up from his chopping, Roberto said, "No rush. I'll take the banana bread out when the timer goes off if you get stuck at the *Chronicle* preaching about the virtues of farm-to-table cuisine."

"Thank you." Amanda nodded. She didn't love the fact that her line cook assumed she was heading to Ryan's office, but at least he'd been kind enough not to mention the kissing.

And the fleeing.

Belle would have surely brought it up again, but she was too busy waiting tables to notice Amanda pouring a cup of coffee and topping it off with a generous dollop of steamed milk. Maybe she could actually sneak out for a minute unnoticed. *Only* a minute—just long enough to deliver the coffee, ask Ryan how things were going with Tucker and smooth things over after her awkward exit from his home the other day. She honestly didn't have time for anything else. The barbecue fundraiser was next weekend and while most of the plans were under control, she still needed to round up a prominent member of the community to judge the cook-off portion of the festival. The trouble was that she'd managed to convince so many local businesses to set up booths at the fundraiser that she hardly knew anyone else she could ask to pitch in.

She'd deal with that later, though. First she needed to apologize for her lack of basic social skills when it came to the opposite sex. At least she wouldn't have to worry about Ryan wanting to kiss her again. The fact that she hadn't heard from him was a pretty good indication that he'd gotten over that particular urge.

She gave the coffee a final stir and fastened a to-go lid on top of the paper cup, but the moment she looked up, she found herself face-to-face with her parents.

"Mom." She glanced back and forth between them. Her mother's smooth, dark skin always contrasted so beautifully with her father's fair complexion. "Dad. What are you doing here?"

Her mother lifted a brow. "Hello to you too, dear."

Amanda shook her head. "Sorry, I just wasn't expecting you. Aren't you supposed to be on a cruise? I thought you were leaving this morning."

Her mom and dad regularly took the grandkids on a Disney cruise this time of year. Of course Alexis and Paul went too. Josh and Amanda routinely got invited, as well, but Amanda couldn't imagine leaving the Grille. Nor could she picture her bachelor brother on a cruise full of children and cartoon characters.

"Little Teddy came down with the chicken pox last night so we had to postpone," her father said.

Amanda gasped. "Oh no! Is he okay?"

"He's cranky as can be. Thank goodness the other five children have already had the chicken pox, or Alexis and Paul would have really had their hands full," her mom said, glancing around the restaurant and frowning slightly when her gaze landed on the specials board. "Since when do we serve a fried green tomato caprese salad?"

Busted.

Inspired by Ryan's positive reaction to the dish, she'd impulsively added it to the menu without consulting her mother. She'd even somehow managed to convince herself she'd done nothing wrong, since she ran the place. But it was still a family-owned establishment, not a sole proprietorship. And Amanda's mom wasn't ready to change things. Amanda's grandmother had written the menu way back when Main Street first got car traffic. Why tinker around with tradition?

Maybe because I'm dying of culinary boredom.

"The customers seem to like it." She lifted her chin. This was it—the moment she'd been preparing for. She needed to convince her parents to let her change things up a bit. She could live without getting into catering if she could at least switch up a dish or two. "Actually, I've been meaning to talk to you both..."

Her voice drifted off as she caught sight of a flash of gray through the window behind her dad's head.

The stray dog!

She'd had her eyes peeled for days and hadn't spotted the animal at all. Now there it was, trotting down the sidewalk as if it were heading to Andy's Antiques to browse through stacks of old china and homespun quilts.

"Just a sec. I'll be right back." She dashed out of the Grille and sprinted after the dog.

The scruffy little pup glanced over its shoulder and picked up its pace, clearly up for a game of chase.

"Stop," Amanda yelled. "I'm trying to help you."

She should have grabbed a handful of meat loaf or something so she could lure the dog closer, but she'd been in such a hurry to bolt after it that instead she'd grabbed the cup of to-go coffee she'd prepared for Ryan. It sloshed in her hand as she rounded the corner toward the Granary in pursuit of the stray.

And then suddenly she was no longer running. The paper cup in her grip seemed to explode, drenching her in Appalachian Breakfast Blend from head-to-toe. Dazed, she wiped the warm liquid from her eyes.

When she opened them, the scruffy gray dog was nowhere to be seen.

But Ryan Carter was gripping her shoulders and looking down at her with a glint of amusement in his eyes. He was holding her exactly the same way he had when he'd plowed into her on the sidewalk last week. In fact, they were standing in almost exactly the same spot where they'd had their previous run-in.

The only thing different was the smile on his lips—
and the fact that she'd kissed those lips just days ago.

His smile broadened, and the coffee cup slipped
from her fingertips. "We've got to stop meeting like
this."

"Oh my God. I just ran straight into you, didn't I?"
Amanda blinked up at Ryan, clearly stunned to find
herself in a second coffee collision with him in just a
matter of days.

Ryan knew how she felt. He was tempted to believe
fate had thrown them together again, but he reminded
himself he didn't believe in the notion.

Still, what were the odds?

"Look at your chest." A flush crept across Amanda's
cheeks, turning her complexion from tawny to scarlet.
"I mean your *shirt*. Look at your shirt. It's a mess."

She dabbed ineffectually at the growing stain on his
blue oxford with the cuff of her cardigan sweater while
Ryan let his gaze travel over her now-familiar features.
God, it was good to see her again. In the days since he'd
kissed her, he'd had to stop himself from contacting
her at least ten times a day. But he knew staying away
was for the best. She'd obviously considered the kiss
a mistake, and he wasn't sure he could look her in the
eye and pretend he agreed.

Yes, the timing had been terrible. But the kiss itself?
Perfection.

"I think I'm making it worse." She quit trying to sop
up the mess and her palms came to rest on his pectoral
muscles. She bit her lip and stared at his drenched torso

for a few long seconds until she seemed to realize she was touching him, and then she took a backward leap and nearly tripped over the curb.

Ryan righted her before she fell. "Easy there."

"Thanks." She straightened, crossed her arms and then recrossed them.

Why did he get the feeling she was trying to stop herself from touching him again?

He bit back a smile. Amanda Sylvester wasn't acting at all like a woman who regretted kissing him. Maybe he'd misconstrued the reason for her hasty departure and her avoidance of him. Then again, what difference did it make? The surprise lip-lock had been a one-time thing. It had to be. As if his plate hadn't already been full enough with Dillon and the new dog, now he had the visit from Finch and Annabelle hanging over his head. He sure as hell didn't need to be kissing a woman he barely knew.

Even if meeting that woman had been the nicest thing that had happened to him a long, long while.

"Your eggs were delicious," he blurted.

Smooth. Real smooth.

"Oh." He watched as her lips curved into a surprised smile, and try as he might, he couldn't stop thinking about the way she'd tasted. So warm. So decadently sweet. "I'm glad you liked them."

"I did, and Dillon devoured them." Ryan shrugged. "I can't get him to eat any of my cooking, other than hot dogs and frozen pizza."

She winced. "No offense, but frozen pizza doesn't qualify as cooking."

He held up his hands. "None taken. That's why I usually stop by to get dinner for us at the Grille."

"Right." Her smile faded. "I noticed you haven't stopped by in a few days, and I know it's my fault. Believe it or not, the coffee I just dumped all over you was supposed to be an apology of sorts."

"You don't owe me an apology. Not at all. But as peace offerings go, throwing it at me like that was certainly a memorable tactic." He grinned, picked the paper cup off the ground and tossed it into the nearby trash can.

"I was chasing a dog—a stray I've seen here a few times. Did you see it? Small, gray, scruffy?"

"I didn't." He looked around, but there wasn't an animal in sight. Just people drifting in and out of the quaint local businesses that made up Spring Forest's downtown area. "But speaking of dogs…"

She pulled a face. "Oh no. Is Tucker still eating your shoes?"

"No, I've managed to nip that in the bud. But the crate training isn't going so well."

Her gaze narrowed. "Let me guess—you caved and started letting him sleep in Dillon's bed?"

"Guilty as charged. How did you know?"

"Because you're a good dad, that's why." She shrugged, oblivious to the fact that her words made his throat close up.

He actually felt weepy almost, all over a silly compliment. Damn it, what was wrong with him?

You're a good dad.

No one had ever called him that before. Not Maggie. Certainly not Annabelle and Finch.

"You're a good dad, but a pushover of a dog owner. I should have checked in on you sooner. It's just…" She took a deep breath.

"I get it. It's okay." He held a hand to his heart. "If you keep helping me with Tucker, I promise I won't kiss you again."

What was he saying?

Her smile froze in place. "Great."

"Great." He nodded.

This isn't what you want.

No, it wasn't. He also wasn't completely convinced it was what Amanda wanted. But it was for the best.

"Can I ask you another favor?" he said before he could stop himself. For crying out loud, he'd just about lost control of the things coming out of his mouth. "My former in-laws are coming to visit, and they don't seem to share your high opinion of my parenting skills. Maybe you could stop by while they're in town?"

She stared at him for a beat, because of course she did. She was practically a stranger, and he'd just asked her to meet his late wife's parents.

"Never mind." He raked a hand through his hair and did his best to pretend he hadn't just stuck his foot in his mouth in such a major way. "It was a crazy idea."

"You really want me there?" she said quietly.

Yes. Very much. If just one person in the room believed in him, maybe it wouldn't be so terrible.

"I do," he said, then hastily added, "as friends, of course."

A flicker of relief passed through her gaze, and for some strange reason, Ryan felt a stab of disappointment deep in his gut.

Friends.

She nodded. "Sure, if you think it would help."

"Great. Thank you. I know I seem to be asking you for a lot of favors lately." He swallowed. "But I don't know many people here yet and…"

And he liked her. He liked her a lot. He just wasn't sure how to articulate his feelings or if he even should.

Amanda nodded and glanced across the street where Birdie and Bunny Whitaker were walking toward The Gilded Rose Tea Room. The wide-brimmed hat on Bunny's head was so large it bordered on comical. They waved and Amanda waggled her fingers in return.

Then she swiveled her gaze back to Ryan. "I'm going to need a favor in return."

"Anything." After all, he was in no position to argue.

"I need a judge for the barbecue cook-off."

"That's it? You want me to gorge myself on barbecue for a day?" He grinned. "I think I can manage it."

"Good. It might be a nice way for you to get to know the townspeople a little more. Plus, I'm kind of desperate." She stuck her hand out for a shake. "So it's a deal?"

"It's a deal." He took her palm in his, but once they'd shaken hands, he kept holding on, so that their fingertips were loosely interwoven.

That's what *friends* were for, right?

Ryan ground his teeth together. He wasn't sure why

that word irritated him so much all of a sudden, especially since he was the one who'd first uttered it.

He just knew that it did.

A lot…probably more than he was willing to admit, even to himself.

Chapter Eight

The days leading up to the barbecue fundraiser passed in a blur. Amanda could have mentally tallied the time any number of ways, but for some ridiculous reason she calculated it in the number of breakfasts she'd delivered to Ryan and Dillon.

She pretended it wasn't weird to keep cooking for them since they'd firmly established the boundaries of their relationship. They were friends, nothing more. Of course they'd somehow ended the conversation about being "just friends" by accidentally holding hands on the sidewalk for all the town to see. And sure, a casual friend might not drop by at seven in the morning with a batch of homemade cinnamon sticky buns, but Amanda couldn't quite help it. Dillon's sweet little face lit up every time she showed up before he left for school. He was talking almost every day now, especially to Tucker. Amanda was teaching him how to give the dog simple commands, like *sit*, *down* and *roll over*. The boy and the dog were adorable together, like two peas in a pod.

And Ryan…

Well, Ryan was *beyond* adorable. But in the name of self-preservation, she pretended not to notice. Just like she pretended she wasn't thinking about their kiss every time she stood in his kitchen. Or that she didn't catch him looking at her sometimes when he thought she didn't notice.

In short, she was doing a lot of pretending. A scary amount, actually. But she didn't have time to dwell on it because there were a million details to take care of if the barbecue cook-off was going to raise enough money to fix the tornado damage at Furever Paws.

So a mere seven breakfasts after Amanda collided with Ryan on the sidewalk for the second time, she found herself standing in the Granary parking lot alongside Birdie and Bunny on the night before the fundraiser, unloading a pile of boxes containing supplies for the following day from the back of her red pickup truck.

"This is unbelievable, dear." Birdie planted her hands on her hips and took in the white tents lined up in neat rows along the empty lot. "I've never seen this space look so good."

The old grain factory had been converted years ago into an open shopping area for local vendors, and on weekend mornings between April and October, they hosted a farmer's market. Amanda had managed to convince the owners of the lot to let her use it for the barbecue fundraiser on Saturday afternoon, starting exactly one hour after the farmer's market closed for the day.

Sure, she could have used the land out at Furever Paws for the event. Between the shelter property and Whitaker acres, there was plenty of space. But she figured the fundraiser would draw more people if it was located smack in the center of town, and more people meant more money for the rescue mission.

Bunny spun in a circle, taking it all in. "The tents are a particularly nice touch. Where did they come from? I always have to wear my sun hat when I come out here for the farmer's market."

"A hardware store in Raleigh is loaning them to us. They sent a few people down here last night to set them up. I thought people might want to stay longer if we have shade, plus now we can have a booth for some of the adoptable pets and we won't have to worry about them getting too hot." While they were raising money, they might as well find homes for some of the animals at the same time. It was a win-win.

"I don't understand how you've had time to get all of this together so quickly." Birdie arched a brow. "Plus, haven't you been spending a lot of time over at Ryan Carter's house lately?"

Amanda bent to rummage through one of the boxes and re-count the red gingham tablecloths she'd packed so she wouldn't have to meet the older woman's gaze. "I've been helping Ryan with Tucker. You know how impossible that dog can be. We don't want him to get returned to the shelter again, do we?"

"Of course not. It's very sweet of you to go the extra mile like that." Birdie's voice carried an unmistakable hint of innuendo, which Amanda ignored. With all of the pretending she'd been doing lately, she was becoming frighteningly good at keeping a poker face.

Birdie and Bunny exchanged a glance, clearly waiting for her to admit there was more to her early morning visits to the Carter house than just dog training. When she refused to elaborate, they sighed and moved on.

"But how have you managed to do all of this and run the Grille at the same time?" Bunny slid one of the boxes into the Granary's storage shed, where they were keeping the cook-off supplies until they could set up after the market closed tomorrow afternoon.

Amanda slid another box in behind it. "Believe it or not, I have a temporary comanager."

Birdie crossed her arms. "It's about time. Who is it?"

"My brother-in-law, Paul." Amanda reached into the bed of her truck for another box.

"How is that possible? Doesn't Paul work full-time in Raleigh? And don't he and your sister have six kids at home? Paul might be the only person in North Carolina who has more on his plate than you do."

"Not right now, thank goodness. My nephew Teddy came down with the chicken pox the night before Paul and Alexis were supposed to take the kids on a cruise with my parents. They've had to postpone the entire trip, but Paul had already arranged to take vacation days from work. He's really not happy with his office job, so when I asked if he could lend a hand at the Grille until I could get this taken care of, he agreed."

Amanda still hadn't gotten up the courage to tell her parents about her dream of branching out into catering, but when she'd returned to the Grille after dashing after the scruffy stray dog the other day, they'd still been there waiting for her. As soon as they'd told her Paul had some time off she'd called him and begged him to help for a few days. Miraculously, he'd actually liked the idea.

"Good for you. We just can't tell you how much we appreciate what you've done," Bunny said.

Birdie nodded, but Amanda held up a hand. "Don't thank me until tomorrow when we've successfully pulled this off. Please."

"Fair enough. Our thanks is officially postponed." Birdie's eyes twinkled in the deepening twilight. Behind her, fireflies glowed in the wooded area adjacent to the Granary. "But, sugar. No matter what happens tomorrow, you know we love you, right?"

Then, before Amanda could prepare herself, Birdie gathered her into a hug. The unexpected contact made her throat clog. Bunny was supposed to be the touchy-feely sister, not Birdie. Birdie was strictly no-nonsense, and Amanda liked that about her. She always knew exactly where she stood with Birdie. The fact that the unflappable woman was now embracing her made Amanda keenly aware of just how much trouble the shelter must be facing.

"I love you too. Both of you, and all the animals too." Even the crazy love-struck Llama Bean, who might have been Amanda's biggest competition for Ryan Carter's heart.

If she'd been interested in him that way.

Which she wasn't.

She swallowed around the lump in her throat and squeezed Birdie in return. When the older woman released her, Amanda figured if she was ever going to press for more information about the shelter's financial problems, now was the time. She really wanted to know what had happened to the insurance policy, but more than that, she needed to know if the situation was even more dire than she realized so she could calculate how much she needed to collect for admission. She'd planned on charging ten dollars a head for entrance to the festival, but she could bump the ticket price up to twelve or fifteen, if necessary.

"Look." She took a deep breath. "I don't mean to overstep, but how has Furever Paws gotten into so much trouble? The tornado damage is bad, but…"

"But our insurance policy should be taking care of it." Birdie nodded. "You don't have to say it. We know. The thing is…"

"You don't have insurance." Amanda winced. "I overheard you both discussing it when I was at the shelter to walk Tucker. I should have told you I knew, but I wasn't sure how to bring it up."

Bunny patted her arm. "It's okay, we don't mind you knowing. The only reason we haven't mentioned it is because the whole thing is just a terrible mistake.

We *had* insurance—had a policy for years—but Gator forgot to make the most recent payment, and he feels awful about it. The poor thing."

"He forgot?" Amanda blinked. "That doesn't sound like Gator."

She'd only met Gator once—a few years ago when he'd come to check out the shelter after Birdie and Bunny made a few improvements to the main building. Once upon a time, he'd owned a quarter of the wooded area that bordered the section of Whitaker acres where the farmhouse stood. When Bunny and Birdie's parents passed away, the land was handed down and split equally between the four siblings—Birdie, Bunny, Gator and their late brother, Moose.

Moose sold his share immediately and left for Florida, where his three kids, Evie, Josie and Grant, currently lived. While Birdie and Bunny hung on to the land they'd inherited, tending to it with loving care, Gator sold his portion the minute the real estate market peaked. According to the Spring Forest rumor mill, he'd invested the proceeds wisely and was now wealthy enough to own a mansion and a yacht that he kept docked at the Outer Banks.

He didn't come around much anymore, but Amanda always assumed it was because he was busy managing his millions up in Durham. Certainly, the Whitaker sisters spoke of him with a great deal of pride. Birdie, in particular, doted on her baby brother. And Amanda knew that Gator was the one they trusted to handle all the money matters, both to keep the shelter running and to manage their private investments, so they'd have enough to live comfortably. Amanda had figured that he must be worthy of that trust.

Now she wasn't so sure.

Maybe Birdie and Bunny shouldn't be putting such blind trust in Gator to run their financial affairs if he couldn't even remember to pay the insurance bill.

Birdie smiled, but it didn't quite reach her eyes. "His business is booming. He's been so busy with his investment firm that he simply forgot. Like Bunny said, he feels terrible about it."

But not terrible enough to pay for the storm damage himself? Shouldn't he have been able to cover it if he was doing as well as his sisters seemed to believe, especially since the lapsed insurance was his fault?

Amanda faked a pleasant expression as best she could. "I'm sure he does. Is he going to make it down for the cook-off tomorrow?"

She wasn't sure whether to hope he was making the trip or not. On one hand, Birdie and Bunny's nephew Grant was coming all the way from Florida to show his support, so of course Gator should make an appearance. Durham was practically right down the highway from Spring Forest.

On the other hand, if Gator did turn up, Amanda might be tempted to strangle him on sight.

"No, I'm afraid not." Birdie shook her head. "He has an important meeting that he can't miss."

On a Saturday. Right. "That's a shame. But don't worry—the event is going to be a huge success. We'll have the money for the storm repairs before you know it."

Amanda hated to make a promise she wasn't sure

she could keep, but she really didn't have a choice. Birdie and Bunny weren't the only ones depending on her—so were all the animals at Furever Paws who were in need of permanent homes. Life had already thrown those sweet pets a disappointing curveball, and then the tornado had been the icing on the cake.

She couldn't let them down.

She wouldn't. They deserved a shelter that was warm and dry.

She'd fire up every grill and smoker in the South if she had to. One way or another, Furever Paws would get its new roof.

It was a good thing Paul had stepped up to the plate at the Grille while he was on vacation, because the morning of the barbecue fundraiser, Amanda was absolutely useless at the diner. She showed up for work, just like every other Saturday of her life, because there was nothing she could do at the Granary until the farmer's market closed up. But she was so distracted that she switched the decaf coffeepot with the caffeinated one, resulting in a very sleepy Doc J, who nearly fell asleep face-first in his pancakes.

That wouldn't do at all. He'd signed on to run a free microchip clinic at the cook-off, and Birdie and Bunny couldn't stop talking about it. Amanda needed him awake and alert.

"Here you go, Doc." She handed him a fresh mug filled to the brim with strong black coffee—fully leaded this time.

He took a fortifying sip and then frowned at her.

"Why don't you sit down? You're going to have a long day, and all this flitting around is making me nervous."

"I'd love to, but I can't. There's too much to do." Like stare out the window for signs of rain. And wonder whether or not the tents were holding up in the cool spring breeze. And fret over whether or not the pit masters from Wilmington would arrive in Spring Forest in time to get their smokers all set up and running.

Worrying about everything that could go wrong was practically a full-time job.

"Amanda, darlin'. Come with me. We need to have a word." Belle grabbed Amanda by the hand and dragged her to the kitchen. Once they were on the other side of the swinging door, she tugged on the strings of Amanda's apron until it floated to the floor.

"What are you doing?" She bent to pick it up, but Belle snatched it away before she could grab it.

She wadded the fabric into a ball and pointed at the back door. "It's *my* turn to fire *you* now. Get out."

Amanda rolled her eyes. "Nice try, but you can't fire me."

"She might not be able to, but I sure can," Paul said as he pushed through the swinging door carrying a tray of empty plates.

"Um, I don't think so. I'm the manager, remember?"

"And I'm the comanager," he retorted. "For a while, anyway."

Point taken. "But…"

"But you're driving us all crazy, sis. I can handle things around here by myself. Isn't that why you asked for my help to begin with?" He set the tray down beside the big industrial sink.

Just as she was about to explain the three-sink dishwashing process to him, he plunged the dirty dishes into the sink on the far left—the proper choice. She paused before answering. "You're doing a pretty incredible job so far. I'm actually kind of stunned."

"Gee, thanks." He arched a brow. "But what are you still doing here? I fired you for the day, remember?"

"Fine." She held up her hands. "I'm going."

Belle winked at Paul. "Thanks. You have no idea how long I've been waiting for her to get a dose of her own medicine."

"I heard that." Amanda grabbed her handbag and slung it over her shoulder. "Promise me all of you will come down to the Granary to help set up by noon? We're closing for the afternoon. Maybe we should put a sign on the door. It could just say Barbecue and have an arrow pointing down the street."

"I'm a step ahead of you, sis. I already made one. Goodbye now." Paul gave her an exaggerated wave.

Okay, then.

Amanda slipped out the back door and closed it firmly behind her. Paul and Belle were right. They could survive without her for half a day. Not spending every spare hour at the Grille was just such a foreign concept, she was having trouble wrapping her mind around it. Even when she'd been hammering out the details for the fundraiser, she'd made all the necessary calls from her tiny office off the kitchen.

She hummed as she rounded the corner onto Main

and checked the sky—yet again—for signs of rain. There wasn't a gray cloud in sight. So far, so good. Maybe she'd go ahead and dash over to the Granary to see if there was anything she could do while the farmer's market was still in full swing.

Somehow, though, when it came time to veer toward the old grain factory, Amanda's feet willfully disobeyed. In just a few short strides, she found herself turning onto the sidewalk that led to Kingdom Creek and a certain homey cottage with a big window in the kitchen that looked out over a backyard with a tire swing.

When she reached Ryan's front porch, the tips of her fingers hesitated over the doorbell. This sort of unannounced visit was different than the little breakfast visits she'd been making every morning. Those encounters had all been preplanned, scheduled events. Not *dates*, obviously. They'd been innocent dog training sessions...with breakfast.

But the addition of sticky buns or homemade butter biscuits drizzled with Carolina honey didn't make the visits into anything remotely date-like. Food was her business, and Ryan was a single dad. He'd come right out and admitted that he was a terrible cook, and he and Dillon needed to eat.

But now here she was, about to ring his doorbell at a random, nonscheduled time without so much as a strip of bacon to serve as a good excuse.

Nope.

Her stomach flipped.

She couldn't do it. She withdrew her hand from the

bell and turned to go, but the front door swung open before she could take a step.

"Going somewhere?" There was a hint of amusement in Ryan's voice, but it still had the deep timbre that always seemed to reach down inside her and make her want to crawl under his covers and ask him to read her a bedtime story.

Because that was a completely normal, *friendly* reaction.

She turned around, face aflame. "Hi."

"Hi, yourself." He opened the door wide, and to her immense relief, he didn't ask what she was doing there unannounced or mention the fact that he'd just caught her on the verge of running away. Again. "Come on in."

She stepped over the familiar threshold and the minute she was inside, Tucker bounded toward her with a sock in his mouth.

"Look at you." She shook her head and scooped him into her arms. "Up to your old tricks."

"I gave him that sock. It belongs to him now, fair and square. He absolutely didn't steal it from the laundry room while running around unsupervised." Ryan crossed his arms and nodded in mock solemnity.

Amanda narrowed her gaze. "Are you lying right now so I won't tease you about being a pushover like most first-time dog owners?"

"Perhaps."

Laugher bubbled up her throat. What had she been so nervous about? They were talking and joking around, like they always did.

Like friends.

Her smile wobbled ever so slightly. Who was she kidding? She didn't want to be Ryan Carter's friend. She wanted more than that…so much more.

She wanted to kiss him again. She wanted to rest her fingertips on his solid wall of a chest and feel the pounding of his heart grow quick as his lips came down on hers. She wanted to slide her hands beneath one of those soft cashmere sweaters he'd taken to wearing and move them along his back until he groaned into her mouth.

She wanted it so badly that she could barely see straight.

She swallowed hard and did her best not to stare at his mouth, failing miserably. "No lectures today, since this isn't an official dog training session."

"No?" He took a step closer to her, searching her gaze. And suddenly any and all traces of amusement in his eyes disappeared, and he was looking at her with an expression so heated, so *aching*, that a lump formed in her throat. "What is it, then?"

How was she supposed to answer that question?

She drew in a long breath. "I thought maybe we could all go to the cook-off together."

She bit the inside of her cheek to stop herself from adding a disclaimer about it being a friendly outing. Surely the words would ring false when he was standing close enough for her to smell the clean, woodsy scent of his aftershave. God, it was heavenly. She almost wanted to ask him what kind it was so she could buy some and spritz it on her pillow at night.

Pathetic.

Was this normal? Did all crushes eventually develop into something this intense? Maybe the intensity of it meant it would burn out quickly...but somehow she doubted it.

"I'd like that very much." He lifted a hand, and at first she thought he was reaching toward the dog in her arms, ready to give Tucker a pat or a scratch on the chin.

But instead, he gently tucked a lock of her hair behind her ear. A shiver coursed through her as his hand came to rest on her neck, and he smiled a smile she'd never seen on his lips before. A knowing smile. A *private* smile, just for her.

It was a gift as precious as a diamond. When he'd first moved to town, Amanda had waited days...weeks...for Ryan Carter to smile at her. Even after she'd begun helping him with Tucker and his trademark brooding expression had relaxed into something far more welcoming, there was still a hesitancy about the way he looked at her. His features were just a tiny bit strained, as if every time he smiled, he felt like he'd been caught doing something he shouldn't.

Not this time, though. Everything about his expression, from the heat in his brandy-hued eyes to the curve of his lips was deliberately welcoming—freely given and so steeped in intention that her heart skittered to a stop.

Ever so slightly, she lifted her mouth toward his. An invitation.

Her subconscious was screaming at her, telling her to stop. *This isn't what friends do.* But it was too late. Her eyes drifted closed, and wild horses couldn't have stopped her from kissing him right then. Nothing could.

Except a certain childish voice.

"Hi, Amanda."

Dillon.

Her eyes flew open, and she barely had time to register the fact that Ryan's mouth was just a whisper away from hers before the two of them leaped apart from one another.

Amanda stumbled backward against the closed door, but managed not to drop poor Tucker, whose furry little head was swiveling back and forth between her and Ryan as if the dog was trying to figure out why they were acting so nutty.

"Hey, bud." Ryan ruffled Dillon's hair. "We didn't hear you coming. You…ah…surprised us."

Understatement.

Amanda had enough trouble letting her guard down long enough to kiss Ryan without an audience. Something told her that doing so in front of his troubled son might not be the best idea in the world.

She didn't know what to say or how to act. For once, she wished she was back at the Grille making her grandmother's flavor-challenged meat loaf recipe that her mom insisted she keep serving.

At the sight of Dillon, Tucker suddenly squirmed to get down, and Amanda was immensely grateful for something to do. She set his wiggling little body on the ground and he scurried toward the boy.

Dillon laughed as the dog threw himself at his feet.

"Maybe we should get going," Ryan said, looking anywhere and everywhere except at her.

She cleared her throat. "Good idea."

After all, wasn't she supposed to be planning a major community event today instead of attempting a make out session with her friend?

Indeed she was.

Chapter Nine

Ryan did what he could to help get everything set up for the barbecue cook-off, but in truth, there wasn't much for him to do. Amanda had organized the event down to the smallest detail. As soon as the farmer's market shut down, business owners from the quaint establishments up and down Main Street flooded the old grain factory to set up booths ranging from a cake walk run by the folks from Great American Bakery to Snap Pop Candy Shop's Wheel of Fortune. Before the event officially started, Dillon had already spun the wheel enough times to win three lollipops and the ultimate treasure—a packet of gummy sharks. Tucker never left his side.

Ryan snapped pictures for the paper and jotted down details in his notepad in case Jonah missed something, but mostly spent the time trying his best to make sense of the almost-kiss with Amanda. The memory of it floated between them, electrifying the air. Whenever Amanda's arm brushed against his and whenever he unexpectedly caught the sound of her laughter above the din of the crowd at the Granary, a shift took place deep in his chest.

He had feelings for her.

There, he'd admitted it. Not aloud, obviously. Only to himself, because he still wasn't in any kind of place to enter into a relationship. The fact that Dillon had nearly walked in on him kissing Amanda had been a wake-up call. A big one. He was supposed to be concentrating on fatherhood. He owed Dillon that much.

But that didn't stop Ryan from thinking about what might have happened if Dillon *hadn't* stumbled upon them earlier in the foyer. Or how nice it felt to walk beside her as she greeted friends at the fundraiser. Or how she shivered every time he touched her. So sensitive. So responsive.

He took a deep breath and reminded himself he was there to supervise Jonah's coverage of the event, and as the judge of the cook-off, not as Amanda's escort. But he couldn't seem to tear himself away, so an hour after the fundraiser officially started, she was still just an arm's length away, beaming at him as she introduced him to various members of the community. And feeding him barbecue.

So. Much. Barbecue.

"We should stop by the Furever Paws adoption tent," she said after Ryan had eaten his fifth plate of pulled pork. It was his job, after all.

He eyed her as he tossed his napkin in the trash. "If you're trying to get me to adopt that llama, the answer is no."

"For the record, Llama Bean is in the petting zoo, not the adoption tent. But we can certainly head over there next if you miss her that badly."

"Can't wait," he said dryly. But he'd promised Dillon he could feed the pygmy goats, so a visit to the petting zoo loomed. Oh boy.

Predictably, the adoption tent was packed. Ryan recognized a lot of the dogs from his recent visit to the shelter, but there were several he'd never seen before. Amanda explained that the shelter only housed pets that didn't have a foster home. She'd invited a lot of the foster families to bring their adoptable pets to the barbecue event, which had apparently been an ace idea. There wasn't a dog in the tent that wasn't currently being oohed and ahhed over.

Ryan nodded toward Tucker trotting at the end of the red leash in Dillon's hand. "Do you think Tucker recognizes any of his friends from his shelter days?"

Amanda shook her head. "Doubtful. Tucker isn't exactly a social butterfly. He likes Dillon and nobody else." A flush crept up her face and she looked away. "Except you."

Ryan didn't know why the odd little dog had chosen the two of them to attach himself to, but he was grateful. So damned grateful…every day. "It's because of you. I haven't forgotten that you're the one who brought Dillon and Tucker together. I won't forget that. Ever."

She turned to face him again and when their eyes

met, everything around them seemed to fade away. They could have been standing alone together in his foyer again, on the verge of kissing, for all the attention he paid to the people and animals around them. The urge to touch her was almost overwhelming. What was happening to him?

Her... Amanda. *She* was happening to him, and trying to ignore the very nonfriendly feelings he had for her was becoming more difficult with each passing day. Case in point: a well-built guy was currently heading her way with a smile on his face as Ryan's gut tightened into a hard knot.

Who was this guy? More important, since when did Ryan get *jealous*?

"Amanda, congratulations." The mystery guy gave her a one-armed hug that didn't seem intimate in any way. Still, the knot in Ryan's stomach showed no signs of dissipating. What the hell was wrong with him?

"This is incredible," he continued. "Everyone in town is here. Birdie and Bunny have got to be thrilled with what you've done here."

"We'll see. I'm still kind of a nervous wreck, and I don't see that changing until we count the proceeds later this afternoon." Amanda glanced back and forth between him and Ryan. "I don't think you two have met, have you? Ryan, this is Daniel Sutton. His law office is just down the street. Daniel, this is Ryan Carter, the new owner and editor-in-chief at the *Chronicle*."

"Hey, man. Nice to meet you." Daniel offered his hand.

Ryan shook it, relaxing a little. He was getting a

definite friend vibe between Amanda and Daniel. Not that it was any of his business. "Same."

Daniel grinned at Dillon, spinning in circles to free himself from Tucker's leash, which had somehow gotten wrapped around his legs. "Is this your boy?"

"Yes. Dillon." Ryan shook his head. "As you can probably tell, we're new dog owners. Neither Dillon nor Tucker has quite mastered the leash yet."

"Give it time." Amanda rested her hand on his forearm before pointing to a trio of little girls busy petting a big brown gentle giant of a dog wearing an Adopt Me vest. "Those are Daniel's daughters, Paris, Penny and Pippa."

Ryan stifled a grin. "Uh-oh. I recognize that look on their faces. It's the same expression Dillon had when he first spotted Tucker. You might be taking that huge dog home with you."

Daniel shook his head. "My housekeeper would murder me. Or worse, she'd quit. And we need her. Truthfully, we need a cook and a nanny too. But most days, I manage on my own. We're always teetering on the verge of chaos, though, and I'm fairly certain adding a one-hundred-pound animal to the mix would mean the end of my sanity."

Ryan laughed. "I hear you."

So Daniel was a single father, too. Interesting. He wasn't sure which seemed more challenging—trying to bond with one withdrawn six-year-old boy or navigating a household of *three* boisterous little girls. They seemed to be competing to see who could lavish the most attention on the dog they were petting. At least they wouldn't be able to sneak up on their father kissing anyone. Daniel could probably hear them coming a mile away.

Ryan glanced at Amanda again, gaze lingering on the tempting pink swell of her lower lip. What had that near-kiss been about, anyway? He was desperate to know. Then again, this wasn't exactly the time or place to figure it out.

He forced his attention back to Daniel, who'd launched into an amusing story about his youngest, Pippa, "borrowing" her classroom's hamster a few weeks ago.

"Long story short—she didn't *borrow* the thing at all. She stole the furry little guy and was keeping him in a plastic carrier under her bed. It was a straight-up kidnapping." He rolled his eyes.

Ryan smirked. "Maybe it's a good thing you're a lawyer."

And maybe he and Daniel needed to be friends. It might be nice to have someone he could talk to about the struggles of parenthood…someone he didn't end up kissing at every turn. Ryan suggested they get a beer together sometime and after Daniel agreed, he rounded up his daughters so he could get back to the Sutton Legal Services tent.

"Well, look at you." Amanda grinned up at Ryan. "Mingling with the community and making friends. Something tells me you and Dillon might end up feeling at home here sooner than you thought you would."

A rush of warmth came over him, aching and sweet. Why was he fighting this? He wanted her. Not just her body, but also her heart. Even if all he could capture was a little piece of it…just enough to make him believe in the hope that glittered in her gaze when she looked at him. He could live a long time on that hope—perhaps even long enough to build a life here. Long enough to stay.

"Maybe we already do," he whispered, brushing his fingertips along the inside of her elbow and reveling in the rush of goose bumps that cascaded over her warm skin.

Then, at last, he gave up the fight. He took her hand in his, lifted it to his lips and pressed a tender kiss to her fingertips right there in the center of Main Street. He was a father but he was also a man. He'd been so sure that going it alone was the right thing to do. In a way, he'd been doing it his whole adult life—even in his marriage. Back then he'd been focused on his career, pushing toward success. Now he was focused on Dillon, and building a connection with his son. They weren't bad goals. But his lone wolf attitude was making everything harder than it needed to be, and he didn't think he could do it anymore. What was he teaching his son by isolating himself from good people?

Let Dillon see that it was okay to need someone.

Let him see his daddy was human.

Let them all see.

"Amanda, I…" He took a ragged inhale.

I'm an idiot. I don't want to be your friend. I want… more.

He might even want everything.

"I know," she murmured, gazing up at him as if she could read his mind. "Me too."

And for a brief, blissful moment, he felt whole again. Healed in a way he hadn't even realized was possible. But the moment ended almost as soon as it had begun when Dillon broke away from the group of kids gathered around the puppy pen and ran toward an older couple picking their way through the crowd and approaching the adoption tent with an unmistakable look of shock on their pale faces. Ryan watched in confusion as his son threw his little arms around their legs, until the awful truth sank in.

Maggie's parents had just shown up unannounced.

Ryan's hand squeezed Amanda's with a sudden death grip and then he released it, shoving his hands into the pockets of his jeans. She felt unmoored for a moment, head spinning with the unmistakable notion that she'd been tossed aside right on the heels of what she thought had been some kind of breakthrough.

Had she only been imagining that look in Ryan's eyes—the one she never thought she'd see? Impossible. She'd seen it…she'd *felt* it, all the way down to her toes. The brooding man who'd swept into her life dressed in a three-piece suit and armor of regret had finally exhaled. Slowly but surely, he'd been vanishing right before her eyes…all this time, all these torturous weeks. And in his place there'd been someone who wanted her too much to pretend otherwise.

Or so she'd thought.

"Annabelle. Finch." Ryan's voice sounded wooden as his gaze swiveled back and forth between the two strangers walking toward them. Dillon trailed after them with Tucker nipping at his heels. "What are you doing here?"

The names sounded familiar, but Amanda couldn't quite place them until the older woman rested a hand on Dillon's shoulder. He looked up at her and smiled in a way that Amanda hadn't seem him do with strangers before. That tiny expression of familiarity was all it took for the significance of what was happening to come crashing down with frightening certainty.

These were Ryan's former in-laws, the Brewsters. They were the source of all the stressful phone calls and the anxiety over their impending visit at the end of the month.

Except they hadn't waited until then, as previously planned. They were right here, right now, and they were looking at Ryan as if he were some kind of monster.

"We thought it best to come right away," Mr. Brewster said. His gaze swept the festival, and then he looked Ryan up and down. "As you know, we've been worried about what kind of environment you've chosen for our grandson. And it appears our concerns were justified. What kind of place is this? Some kind of mangy-looking camel just spit on Annabelle."

It had to have been Llama Bean, although she normally didn't spit at people. Most llamas didn't unless they were feeling particularly threatened. Then again, maybe Llama Bean somehow sensed Annabelle Brewster's hostility toward Ryan and stood up for him the only way she knew how.

Amanda had never related so much to a llama in her life. She cleared her throat. "Actually, it was probably a llama. They're related to camels, though. So, good guess."

Finch and Annabelle both looked at her as if she'd just sprouted two heads. Ryan pinched the bridge of his nose and closed his eyes as if he wanted to disappear.

"Um." Why, oh why, had she opened her big mouth? "We don't normally have farm animals in the center of town, I assure you. This is a special occasion."

Mrs. Brewster rolled her eyes, while her husband narrowed his gaze at Amanda. "And you are?"

"Amanda Sylvester. You're Dillon's grandparents, right? It's wonderful to meet you both." She smiled as wide as she could manage. Maybe Dillon's grandparents simply needed a big dose of Southern charm.

Or maybe not.

Neither of them returned the greeting, opting to study her as if she were a science experiment instead.

Ryan's hand moved to the small of her back, but the gesture felt stiff all of sudden. Cold. "Amanda has been helping us out with our new dog. She volunteers at the animal shelter. She's a good friend."

A weight settled instantly on her heart, even though she knew she had no real reason to be upset. Ryan had warned her that the Brewsters were difficult people. They clearly didn't trust Ryan with his own son, much less a stranger who'd just entered their lives—a stranger who they probably suspected might be interested in taking over their late daughter's role in Dillon's life.

But that was ridiculous. Amanda had no intention

of replacing Maggie, either as Ryan's wife or Dillon's mother.

Then why does that friend *label sting so much?*

"I like Amanda. She's nice," Dillon said.

"I like you too." Amanda grinned. Even though he'd been talking on a daily basis since bringing Tucker home, she knew Ryan still tried to praise or encourage him in some way every time he spoke.

Finch and Annabelle clearly weren't the warm and fuzzy type, but she half expected them to do the same. After all, as far as she knew, they hadn't heard their grandson speak in months.

They didn't, though. Instead, Annabelle reached into her purse for a tissue and tried to clean the barbecue sauce off Dillon's face.

"You're a mess, child." She cut her gaze to Ryan, and the set of his jaw hardened into stone. "Honestly, Ryan. You let him run around like this?"

Finch huffed out a sigh. "Were you even aware he needed cleaning up? You weren't keeping an eye on him at all just now. He could have been running around wild for all the attention you were paying to him."

Why wasn't Ryan defending himself? These people were being so unfair.

It's not your business. Stay out of it.

She couldn't, though. She cared too much about Ryan and Dillon to stand there and listen to the Brewsters say things that weren't true. She wished Dan Sutton was still there to jump to Ryan's defense. He was a lawyer, after all. Even Birdie and Bunny would have been helpful at the moment. Anyone.

But the last time she'd spotted the Whitaker sisters had been back at Doc J's microchip clinic, and from the look of things they'd been enjoying the vet's company far too much to wander elsewhere. Bottom line—there was no one else who could defend Ryan. Everyone else in the tent was fawning over a dog, oblivious to the family drama unfolding in their midst. If anyone was going to speak up, it would have to be her.

"But Dillon was right there at the puppy pen." Amanda waved toward the corner of the tent where most of the small children had gathered to watch the youngest adoptable pups romp and play. "Ryan was watching him. I was too."

"Amanda, it's okay," Ryan said. "You don't have to say anything. Finch and Annabelle can come back to the house, and we can get this sorted out."

"Amanda can come home too," Dillon chimed in. "She can make us breakfast tomorrow, like she always does."

All the breath left Amanda's body in one rapid whoosh. *Oh God.* Why did her little breakfast routine sound so scandalous all of a sudden?

Probably because it makes it sound like I'm living *at Ryan's house instead of stopping by every day before school.*

The Brewsters both glared at her. Yep, that's exactly what they thought. They were probably picturing her frying up eggs in a satin negligee instead of ringing the doorbell at seven in the morning wearing jeans and her Main Street Grille T-shirt.

Finch lifted an accusatory brow. "Is this true, Ryan?"

Amanda shook her head. "It's not quite how it sounds."

Ryan's eyes went dark—darker than she'd ever seen them before. "My relationship with Amanda isn't any of your business, Finch."

Mr. Brewster's mouth hung open for a second before finally closing. Amanda's legs turned to water. What was Ryan doing? He'd just told them they were friends. *Good* friends, but still. That wasn't quite the same thing as letting them believe she regularly slept over at his house.

Especially since she'd *never* spent the night with Ryan before.

For reasons she couldn't quite identify, she had the definite feeling that she never, ever would. Even more puzzling, that realization left her suddenly heartsick.

"I'm sorry, but I need to check on a few things." Amanda turned toward Finch and Annabelle. "Again, it was lovely meeting you. I hope you enjoy your time in Spring Forest."

Ryan's gaze fixed with hers, pleading with her. Begging her not to leave.

She shook her head. *I can't be here.* This discussion had nothing to do with her. Whatever was going on between Ryan and his in-laws was personal family business. And as she was so painfully aware, she and Ryan weren't family.

She wasn't sure what they were at all anymore.

Chapter Ten

"Are you okay?" Mollie McFadden caught Amanda by the sleeve as she hustled past the Best Friends Dog Training booth.

She stopped, glanced over her shoulder and took a breath.

When she'd left Ryan, Dillon and the Brewsters behind at the adoption tent, she hadn't been headed anywhere in particular. The line she'd given them about announcing the winner of the cook-off had been a white lie. As the event judge, Ryan had already made his decision, but Amanda wasn't scheduled to present the winner with the trophy for another forty-five minutes. She'd just needed to get away, and since Mollie's dog training stall was clear on the other side of the Granary, it seemed as good a place to stop as any.

Plus, she could use a friendly face right now, and Mollie's definitely fit the bill.

"I'm fine." Amanda shrugged and wrapped her arms around her middle.

Hold it together. You're in charge of this entire event. You can fall apart tonight after you get home.

Mollie's gaze narrowed. "Are you sure? You look a little freaked out and you were running past here almost as quickly as the dog I was trying to catch this morning."

Amanda gasped. "Oh, was it a scruffy gray dog? Smallish?"

"Yeah. How did you know?" Mollie glanced at her booth, where Zeke Harper was handing brochures to people interested in her training classes.

"Because I've seen that dog three times now. I chased him down Main Street the other day. He's quick."

"Right," Mollie said, gaze lingering on Zeke. "Well, I left some dry dog food out on my property. Hopefully he'll come back and I can gain his trust. If not, I'll set out a humane trap and we can get him cleaned up and placed in a home."

"Sounds like a plan." If anyone could get her hands on the stray, it was Mollie. She was great with animals—the best, really.

She had such a good rapport with them, in fact, that she'd confided in Amanda a time or two that she wished she got along as well with people as she did with dogs—especially Zeke Harper.

Not that they weren't friendly with one another.

They were *too* friendly, which was precisely the problem. Zeke thought the world of Mollie, the younger sister of his late best friend. The trouble was that now that Patrick was gone, he seemed to think it was his job to step into the role of big brother rather than love interest.

As if on cue, Zeke looked up and shot Mollie a thumbs up. She grinned at him, but he'd already redirected his attention toward a pretty blonde who'd stopped by the booth.

Mollie sighed. "He'll never see me as anything but a little sister, will he?"

Doubtful. Their history was...*complicated*, for lack of a better word. And Amanda had a newfound appreciation for just how miserable *complicated* felt. "I don't know, but you deserve someone who really appreciates you. Let me set you up with somebody."

Mollie rolled her eyes. "Who with? I'm pretty sure I know every male in Spring Forest, dogs included."

"Fair point." Amanda laughed, but her smile died on her lips at Mollie's next statement.

"I guess there's the new grumpy guy at the paper, though. What's his name again? Ryan something?"

"Carter," she said quietly. "Ryan Carter."

"Why do you sound so weird all of a sudden?" Then her eyes widened and her mouth curved into a grin. "I see. You like him, don't you?"

Amanda's cheeks blazed with heat.

Mollie nodded. "Yep, I'm right. I can't believe I forgot how much you love the quietly cranky type.

He's basically Tucker in human form. You're perfect for each other."

Perfectly hopeless, maybe.

She forced a smile and realized she'd been doing that a lot lately. "On that note, I need to go announce our winner."

"Sure you do." Mollie winked.

Amanda gave her a final wave before she headed toward the food vendors, but Mollie was too busy mooning over Zeke to notice.

She sighed. Mollie had known Zeke for years. Was that where Amanda's crush on Ryan was headed? Toward months, maybe even *years*, of heartbreak?

No, thank you. She couldn't do it. She should probably just keep her distance from him from now on. Surely she'd get her head out of the clouds eventually. If anything, maybe she could manage to convince everyone that she didn't have a thing for cranky members of the opposite sex—her devotion to Tucker notwithstanding. If she truly found grouchiness sexy, she'd have probably ended up with Cade Battle, co-owner of Battle Lands Farm, where she liked to buy grass-fed beef and free-range eggs for the Grille. Cade ran the farm along with his brother and father, who seemed like truly lovely people. Somehow the niceness gene must have skipped Cade because he didn't seem to possess a personable bone in his body.

The Whitaker sisters seemed to adore him, though, much to Amanda's mystification. As the closest neighbor to their farmhouse, he'd helped them out many times, so Amanda had been able to twist his arm to get him to show up today to sell produce with his dad. Their booth was on the way to the cook-off area, so when she walked past, she gave Cade a flirty little wave, just to test Mollie's theory.

He frowned and refused to wave back. No shocker there. What's more, Amanda didn't feel even the slightest flicker of attraction. Ha! She knew she didn't have some weird attraction toward distant, brooding men.

Just one *distant, brooding man.*

Her throat clenched. Why did everything always seem to come back to Ryan Carter?

She wasn't sure she wanted to know the answer to that question, and luckily, she wasn't forced to dwell on it any further because a tall, curvy woman with a huge smile on her face was headed her way, waving enthusiastically.

"Amanda?" she said, bouncing toward her. "Amanda Sylvester? That's you, right?"

Amanda nodded. "The one and only."

"I'm Rebekah Taylor, the new shelter manager out at Furever Paws. Maybe Birdie and Bunny mentioned me?"

"They did. They're so excited to have you." Birdie and Bunny had hired Rebekah to replace their former manager, who'd moved to Raleigh shortly before the tornado swept through town, but she'd had to give two weeks' notice at her former job before starting at Furever Paws.

Amanda winced. "We're all just so sorry you're starting when the shelter is such a mess. Hopefully we'll raise enough money today to put a dent in the bills for repairs."

"That's why I came to find you. I tried to catch up with you over at the adoption tent, but one minute you were there, and the next minute you weren't." She glanced toward the adoption area, and even though Amanda tried her best not to follow her gaze, she couldn't help it. But a single glance was all it took to confirm what she already knew—Ryan and Dillon were gone. "Anyway, I've been keeping a running tally of the money coming in. Between ticket sales, the barbecue cook-off, the other food booths, the big raffle and silent auction, plus the games and donations, the event has taken in just over twenty thousand dollars so far."

Amanda's breath caught in her throat. "Are you sure? If that's true, we've raised enough to fix the storm damage."

"I know. You did it, girl!" Rebekah threw her arms around Amanda, and Amanda hugged her back.

Tears welled in her eyes. Finally, something good had happened.

Sometimes it seemed as if the tornado had swept through town and turned everything in Amanda's life upside down. She couldn't seem to get anything back on track. But at least Birdie and Bunny could fix their roof and the animals at Furever Paws would have a clean, dry place to stay. The entire town had come together to help, and they'd done it. They'd saved the shelter.

Amanda squeezed her eyes closed tight, but it was no use. She was crying in earnest now, and even though she had every reason to be thrilled, she couldn't quite tell if her tears were happy ones or if they were sad tears.

Somewhere deep down, she suspected they were both.

The following day, Ryan went for a run on the treadmill in the room he'd set up as his home office, just as he always did first thing in the morning. Then he took a shower and got dressed while Tucker ran off with his dirty socks, which had also become a regular part of his morning routine.

Dillon slept in, as he usually did on Sunday mornings, but Ryan kept a constant eye on the clock to make sure he'd be ready by seven in case Amanda dropped by for their usual dog training session.

He hadn't heard a word from her since their awkward encounter with Finch and Annabelle at the cook-off the day before. Granted, he hadn't called her, either. But he'd spent most of the afternoon and evening trying to convince his former in-laws that Dillon was doing fine in Spring Forest. More than fine, actually. Since they'd adopted Tucker, Dillon had been thriving.

Ryan had driven them past Dillon's school and the park where they liked to take Tucker for walks. He'd shown them the crayon drawings Dillon had brought home from class. They were whimsical, colorful depictions of the things that mattered most to him in this new place they called home—Tucker curled into a ball on his dog bed, Dillon's dinosaur toy, Ryan holding him tight in the bathtub as a tornado raged outside the house. That last one put a lump in Ryan's throat every time he saw it. Not only because it reminded him of the very real danger they'd faced the night of the storm, but because for possibly the first time ever, he'd been there when his son really needed him. Ryan had never been a star player in any of Dillon's crayon drawings in Washington.

Now he was. And that meant more to him than any of the Pulitzers he'd won during his tenure at the *Post*.

His in-laws hadn't been overtly impressed with any of it, though. They'd sat quietly through Ryan's tour and politely refused his suggestion that they stop by the Grille for dinner once the barbecue cook-off had ended and the businesses up and down Main Street reopened. But nor had they been as openly hostile as they'd acted at the fundraiser. It wasn't exactly a cause for celebration, but Ryan took his victories where he could get them.

Everything was going to be fine. Now that Finch and Annabelle had seen Dillon—now that they'd heard him *speak*—they'd stop worrying so much. Ryan had offered to let them sleep in his bedroom while he took the couch, but didn't argue when they'd insisted on driving to Raleigh and spending the night in a hotel.

And that was great because he desperately hoped to see Amanda on his doorstep, bright and early, just like always. She'd obviously been rattled by the way Finch and Annabelle had acted, and he couldn't blame her. Ryan hadn't exactly behaved like a gentleman either. Seeing them had been such a shock that he'd been stunned into silence as they'd railed against Spring Forest, against *her*.

He wanted...*needed*...to make things right, so he did the only thing he figured might do the trick. He decided to make her breakfast.

She was always cooking for him and Dillon, not because he'd asked her to, but because it was her way of showing she cared. But no one ever cooked for her, and it was time that changed.

The only breakfast dish he might be able to pull off with any success was pancakes. By some stroke of luck, he had a box of Bisquick in the cabinet and a bottle of maple syrup in the fridge that he kept on hand for Dillon's frozen waffles. By quarter to seven, he'd managed to mix up the batter. At six fifty, he flipped the first pancake over in the pan.

The initial attempt wasn't pretty. The pancake came out misshapen, raw in the center and nearly black on the outside. But each one improved just a little bit more, and by seven o'clock he'd successfully plated a short stack that seemed edible.

Ryan set the pancakes in the center of the kitchen table alongside the syrup, which he'd remembered to warm in the microwave, and a sinking feeling came over him when he realized the time was now five after seven. On any other day, he wouldn't have thought anything of it. Sometimes Amanda ran late. But he couldn't help but wonder if he'd messed things up so badly that she wasn't coming back.

He closed his eyes and gripped the edge of the table. *Please.*

His heart thudded dully in his chest as the minutes

ticked by, and right when he was about to give up hope, the doorbell rang.

"Coming." He flew to the door, ready to apologize. Ready to tell her he'd meant the things he couldn't quite articulate the day before. He wanted her in his life, not just as a friend but as something more. If she wanted that too, great. Perfect. But if she didn't, he was willing to take whatever he could get.

He just couldn't face the thought of never seeing her again.

"Surprise. I cooked breakfast." He felt like a love-sick teenager as he swung the door open.

But the light, heady sensation was replaced by confusion when he realized the person standing on his welcome mat wasn't Amanda, after all. Nor was it one of his in-laws. It was a young man he'd never seen before—twentyish maybe, with a beard and black-rimmed glasses.

Ryan frowned. "I think you've got the wrong address."

Why would a stranger be ringing his bell at this early hour? Was door-to-door solicitation even a thing anymore?

"Ryan Carter?" The young man arched a brow.

"Yes." Ryan nodded, but the second the word left his mouth, bile rose to the back of his throat.

Something wasn't right.

The stranger handed him an envelope. "You've been served."

Ryan's grip began to tremble violently as he watched the stranger walk down the sidewalk, climb into a beat-up Volkswagen van and drive away. Something was definitely wrong. Very, very wrong.

He stared at the manila envelope. He knew without a doubt what was inside—notice of a lawsuit. He'd been served with enough cease-and-desist motions at *The Washington Post* to know what had just happened. Politicians and their ilk were quite litigious, probably because most of them had been practicing lawyers before entering public office.

This didn't have anything to do with a story, though. He hadn't written a thing for *The Spring Forest Chronicle* that would anger anyone to this degree.

Still, he clung to hope that there was a simple explanation. He grabbed onto the envelope so hard that he clawed it open instead of gently lifting the flap. But one look at the document inside confirmed his deepest fear, his absolute darkest nightmare.

Motion to Modify Custody of Dillon Carter.

Finch and Annabelle were going to try to take away his son.

Chapter Eleven

Amanda positioned her phone over the plate on the Grille's stainless steel kitchen counter and snapped a picture. She took a few more, just to be safe, zooming in to capture the texture of the food and minimizing the shadows as best she could.

As she scrolled through her image library to choose the one that was the most Instagram-worthy, Paul abandoned his post at the fry station to peer over her shoulder.

"That one looks good." He pointed to the picture Amanda was already leaning toward—an aerial shot of the plate. The bird's-eye view pictures always ended up being her favorites. "But can I ask what on earth you're doing?"

Instinct told her to click her phone off, shove it in

the pocket of her apron and fake a reason to go up front and check on Belle and the other servers in the dining room. No one in her family knew about her Instagram account. She couldn't even get her parents on board with adding a few new recipes to the menu. If they knew about the lofty catering goals she had for the Grille, they'd think she'd lost her mind. When was she supposed to do something like cater a wedding when she had to run the diner? Since her mom and dad had retired to help with the grandkids, they'd come to rely on her to keep the family business running smoothly. But they still liked to be involved, even more so since Amanda's grandmother passed away last year. Amanda's mom had grown up working alongside her mother at the Grille, and keeping the restaurant exactly the same as she remembered it gave her a great sense of comfort. Amanda had learned that lesson the hard way when she'd ordered napkins in a new color and her mom had nearly cried when she'd seen them.

But she couldn't lie to Paul. He'd been so great the past few days. If he hadn't stepped up to help her out during his vacation, there's no way she would have been able to give the fundraiser the attention it needed to make enough money to cover all the storm damage at Furever Paws. So she took a deep breath, tapped her Instagram icon and held up her iPhone for inspection.

He took the cell from her hand and quietly clicked on a few of the individual pictures while Amanda's heart lodged in her throat. Why wasn't he saying anything?

When it seemed as if he'd studied every image on

the page, he finally looked up. A huge smile spread across his face. "These are fantastic, sis."

She released a breath she hadn't realized she'd been holding. "Thanks."

"The recipes are so creative—classic Southern dishes with an upmarket twist." He handed her the phone and pointed at the dish on the counter. "What's this one?"

"Crostini topped with green beans, caramelized onions and bacon."

His eyebrows lifted. "So basically a fancy version of traditional green bean casserole."

"Exactly, only as an appetizer." She pushed the plate toward him. "Try one."

He popped one of the tiny pieces of toast in his mouth and let out a moan as he chewed. "My God, sis. That's delicious."

"Thank you." She beamed.

"What are you planning on doing with all of these lip-smacking creations? Are you writing a cookbook or something?"

"No." But that wasn't such a terrible idea. "I was hoping to eventually talk Mom and Dad into letting me start a catering offshoot of the Grille. We could do local weddings and maybe even branch out and cater some of the high-end parties in Raleigh. What do you think?"

He snagged another crostini and said, "I think it's a great idea, but you know your folks will never go for it. Especially your mom. She's all about keeping the Grille the same and honoring family tradition."

Amanda deflated a little. She wasn't sure until just

then she'd been hoping Paul would somehow convince her that she was wrong about her mom and dad—that they'd get behind her dream. "That's what I thought. Great. I suppose this entire experiment has been a colossal waste of time."

He shook his head. "Why would you say that? You'd be an amazing caterer. The dishes you've come up with are unique and familiar at the same time. That seems like a perfect hit for the wedding and gala crowd to me."

"But Mom and Dad will never agree. You said so yourself."

He shrugged. "They won't want it to be part of the Grille, but why does it have to be? Do it on your own. It's your baby."

Right. Like she could start a new business on the side while she ran the Grille six days a week.

She cast a wistful glance at her Instagram profile page. She was up to almost nine thousand followers. Not exactly food goddess Chrissy Teigen-level numbers, but not bad either. Paul resumed his spot at the fry station and Amanda polished off a few more of the crostinis until Belle swished through the door with an uncharacteristically serious look on her face.

"What is it?" Amanda's hand paused midway to her mouth. A lone green bean fell onto the counter.

Note to self: don't pile the appetizers quite so high... when and if I ever get to serve them to anyone.

"You need to come up front." Belle sighed. "Ryan is here."

"Oh." She set down the crostini and stared at it so she wouldn't have to meet Belle's gaze.

Amanda had been doing her best to give Ryan space since the Brewsters had shown up unannounced. She figured it was the right thing to do. But the barbecue fundraiser had been four days ago, and she had no idea whether the older couple was still in town or if they'd gone back to Washington. And if she was really being honest with herself, she was hurt that she hadn't heard from Ryan at all. She knew he'd probably been overwhelmed, but after all, he'd been the one to ask her for moral support when his in-laws came to visit. That had been his idea, not hers.

Was it so crazy that she'd expected an invitation of some sort? To lunch, dinner…anything?

Her phone had been conspicuously silent, so she'd spent the past few days trying to stay as busy as possible so she wouldn't have time to dwell on whatever mixed-up feelings she had for Ryan and his adorable household.

She'd missed him, though. Dillon and Tucker too.

"Did he ask for me?" she said, hating the telltale tremor in her voice.

"No, not exactly." Belle let out a long breath. "But he looks like a wreck. Something is wrong. I think you should go out there."

Paul glanced up, but said nothing. Having another guy around the Grille was nice, since Paul never commented on her nonexistent love life. Still, she couldn't help but wonder if he was reporting everything back to her sister, who would in turn fill their parents in on everything. Oh well, having a family spy in her midst was a small price to pay for finally having some help. Even if the help was only temporary.

"Fine. I'll do it." Amanda removed her apron and smoothed down her Grille T-shirt.

On the way out the door, she grabbed the plate of leftover crostini. Maybe she and Ryan needed a shield of food between them since every time they were around one another, they couldn't seem to keep their hands to themselves. And thus far, those incidents had only led to trouble.

"Hi," she said with false cheer, sliding across from Ryan in the booth where she found him sitting in the far corner of the restaurant. She'd been aiming for care-free, but the sudden knot in her stomach made that pretty much impossible.

"Hi." His mouth twitched into a weak attempt of a grin.

Belle was right. He looked horrible. His jaw was covered in several days' worth of stubble and his eyes were red-rimmed, as if he hadn't slept in a week.

"Are you okay?" She swallowed. "Has something happened to Dillon?"

"No." He shook his head. "Not yet, anyway."

Amanda stared at the plate of appetizers on the table between them, doing her best to calm her frantic pulse. "You're scaring me."

"Sorry." He raked a hand through his hair. "I didn't want to say anything. I don't want you to worry. I'm meeting Dan Sutton to go over some things, and he asked if we could meet here. It seemed like a good idea at the time."

"Oh," she said quietly.

So Ryan definitely hadn't come to the Grille to see her. He was only there because Dan had suggested it.

She didn't want to be upset. Clearly Ryan was dealing with something major, but at the same she couldn't help feeling a tiny bit wounded that he'd chosen to confide in Dan instead of her. He barely knew Dan Sutton.

"Sorry, I thought..." Her face burned with humiliation. "Never mind. I've got plenty to keep me busy in the kitchen. Have a nice lunch."

She moved to scoot out of the booth, but Ryan caught her hand. "Wait."

"It's okay. Really." The door to the diner chimed as a new customer entered the building. "Dan's here. I'll let you two chat."

Ryan's gaze shifted toward Dan and then back to her. "He's not here as my friend. He's here as my lawyer."

Amanda froze and blinked up at him, afraid to ask him to elaborate. Somehow she knew he hadn't reached out to Dan for help with estate planning or handling a traffic ticket.

"Maggie's parents are suing me for custody of Dillon."

Ryan hadn't meant to blurt out the news like that. He really hadn't.

He'd decided not to tell Amanda about the lawsuit at all—not because he wanted to keep it a secret from her, but because he feared she might blame herself, at least partially, for setting the Brewsters off. The trouble was that he couldn't look her in the eye and lie to her, so he'd kept his distance.

And he'd never been so miserable in his life.

He missed seeing her every day. He missed her smile. He missed tasting her…touching her. His life felt empty without her in it. God help him if he ended up losing Dillon too. He'd never survive it.

"No." She shook her head. Every drop of color drained from her beautiful face. "How could they do this? *Why?* On what grounds?"

"It's all about me. They say I'm a bad influence. A neglectful parent."

She looked at him with such sympathy in her amber eyes that he had to turn away lest he break down.

Her hand came to rest on his forearm. "Ryan, you know that's not true, right?"

He didn't, and that was the worst part about the entire ordeal.

Maggie's death had been a wake-up call. In the dark days following her accident, Ryan had watched his son retreat into a shell of silence, knowing all the while that it was his fault. If he'd taken the time to develop any kind of relationship with Dillon before Maggie died, he'd have been able to comfort him. But he hadn't. He'd been too caught up with his job to give his boy the love and attention he needed. That he *deserved*.

Had he been a bad influence? Hell yes, he had.

But he wasn't anymore. Dillon was his entire world

now, but that didn't matter. It was too little too late—at least according to Finch and Annabelle.

"Ryan, good to see you." Dan stood beside the booth, wearing a conservative suit and holding a briefcase. It was a sharp contrast to the casual attire he'd been wearing on Saturday at the barbecue.

The lawyerly clothes were a comfort to Ryan, though, for the way they made the other man look professional and capable. Maybe, just maybe, he'd be able to help. "Dan."

"Sorry. I'll give you two some privacy." Amanda slipped out of the booth, tugging her hand free.

Ryan hadn't even realized he'd still been holding on to it.

He wished he could ask her to stay. God, how he wished. But he had no right to ask her for such a thing. She wasn't his wife. She wasn't even his girlfriend.

"How are you holding up?" Dan asked, taking Amanda's place across from him.

"Not well."

"I can see that. You look like hell." Dan gave him a reassuring smile. "Try not to panic, okay? I'm here to help."

"I can't make any promises. Panic is my default state at the moment."

"I get it." Dan paused, nodding politely at Amanda as she slid two glasses of water in front of them. After she'd gone, he continued. "But I want you to remember one very important thing—grandparents have no legal right to see their grandchildren, much less a legal right to custody."

Ryan remembered hearing something to this effect when he'd been working on a legal story for the *Post* in his early days as a reporter. "Then how is this happening?"

Dan shrugged. "They can file all the paperwork they want, but it doesn't mean they'll get anywhere once the case is in front of a judge."

"I guess I still don't understand why an attorney would even take their case if they have no legal grounds for custody."

"That's a good question. Their lawyer's strategy is obviously to put you in a very poor light. If they can show the court you're unfit to be Dillon's father, it might pave the way for you to lose custody. If that happens, the judge could choose to grant them temporary custody of Dillon instead of turning him over to foster care."

"Foster care?"

What the hell?

Any relief that Dan's encouraging words had prompted in Ryan vanished immediately. The thought of losing Dillon to the Brewsters was bad enough. He couldn't even conceive of turning his son over to strangers.

"That can't happen," he ground out. "It absolutely cannot."

"It won't. I'm prepared to fight this," Dan said firmly.

Ryan nodded and took a gulp from his water glass. Amanda glanced at him from across the room and headed back toward the table, pitcher in hand.

"Look, all we need to do is show that you're a competent, caring father." Dan gave him a meaningful look. "Which you are. This won't be a problem. We'll get letters from Dillon's teacher stating you're actively involved in his education. A few statements from town leaders or business owners testifying that you're an upstanding member of the Spring Forest community wouldn't hurt either. Is there anyone in particular that you'd say is familiar with your parenting style? A friend or family member who can give a detailed account of your good relationship with your son?"

"There might be someone." Ryan's gaze shifted to Amanda, who'd just approached the table to refill his glass.

Once it was full, she straightened with the pitcher and looked back and forth between them. "Would you like anything else? Coffee? Lunch? I told Belle I'd be your server so you could discuss...business...without worrying about interruptions."

"Thank you," Ryan said.

Dan's gaze cut to Amanda and then back at him. "She knows about the lawsuit?"

Ryan nodded. "Amanda's a good friend."

He ground his teeth together as he remembered he'd used those exact words to describe her to Maggie's parents. It hadn't been a lie, but it hadn't necessarily been the truth either. Not the whole truth.

Amanda was more than a friend. He just wasn't precisely sure *how much* more.

Dan's face lit up. "Wait. Are you two dating?"

Amanda blurted out an answer quicker than Ryan could form a response. "No."

Ryan cleared his throat. "I was going to say *not yet.*"

Her lips curved into a shy smile.

Dan's brow furrowed. "It sounds like you two have some things to work out. In any case, too bad. A steady girlfriend—or better yet, a fiancée—would go a long way in showing the judge that you're committed to the relationships in your life. Plus judges always prefer it when a child has a maternal figure living in the house, or at least spending a lot of time there."

"Really?" Amanda's knuckles went white as she continued gripping the water pitcher. "It makes that much of a difference?"

Dan shrugged. "It oftentimes does. You'd be surprised."

Amanda fixed Ryan with a pointed stare. She was looking at him the same way she looked at Tucker when she gave the dog a command and expected him to obey.

Ryan narrowed his gaze. "Whatever you're thinking, the answer is no. You've already done more for Dillon and me than I can possibly repay you for."

"That's what friends are for." She smiled sweetly at him. Too sweetly. Then she turned her attention back to Dan. "So what you're saying is that if Ryan and I were engaged, this whole custody suit might get dismissed more quickly than if he was just a regular single dad."

"That's exactly what I'm saying."

"Again, we're not engaged." He'd never even taken her on a real date. Not once. Though he definitely intended to once Dillon's custody was settled.

But he couldn't think about that now. He was in complete and total survival mode at the moment. Ryan had always been good at compartmentalizing, but even in his current state of desperation, somewhere in the back of his mind, he knew better than to let Amanda get more involved with the lawsuit than she needed to be. What they had was special, and he didn't want to ruin it before it even began.

"But we *could* be engaged." She jammed a hand on her hip, and Ryan knew he was in trouble. "Not for real, I mean. Just temporarily…for the lawsuit."

Dan blew out a breath. "I'm going to stop you right there. You can't lie under oath. You're either engaged or you're not."

"Okay, then." Amanda plunked the pitcher down on the table with a determined thud. "Ryan, will you marry me?"

Chapter Twelve

Ryan lifted the final corner of his sofa cushion, pulled a fitted sheet over it and then eyed Amanda as he smoothed down the covers. "Are you absolutely sure about this?"

"Believe it or not, I've slept on a sofa before. I know how it's done." She glanced at him before quickly averting her gaze, a new habit she'd seemed to develop after she'd spontaneously proposed to him at the Grille. Ryan didn't think she'd looked him properly in the eyes a single time since she'd arrived earlier this evening with an overnight bag slung over her shoulder.

"You know that's not what I meant." He kept his tone gentle, as if he were speaking to a spooked animal. "And besides, you're not crashing on the sofa. I am."

She blinked in the general direction of his forehead.

"I'm not going to toss you out of your bed. I'll be fine out here."

"Please." Ryan rolled his eyes. "What kind of gentleman would I be if I let my future wife sleep on the couch?"

"Fake future wife," she corrected. "It's all for show, remember? We're not actually going through with it. We just need to keep that little secret to ourselves so Dan's conscience is clear. He doesn't want either of us perjuring ourselves."

"But you're fine with it?" Ryan took a step closer—so close that she didn't have any choice but to look at him. Really look. "You're not going to have any problem lying to the judge?"

She lifted her chin. "None whatsoever. Not if it means Dillon gets to stay with you."

He sighed.

He didn't believe her for a minute. She was a terrible liar—and she wouldn't spontaneously get better at it just because she was lying for a noble cause.

Amanda was only trying to help. Of course he knew that. But he didn't feel right pretending they were planning on getting married. Given the delicate state of their budding relationship, it seemed like a really, *really* bad idea.

Did they even have a relationship anymore? Or was this fake engagement the nail in the coffin of romantic involvement? What would happen if he kissed her, right here, right now?

He let out a slow, labored breath. Kissing was definitely off the table. It was going to be torturous enough knowing she was sleeping in his bed with her head on his pillow and her long, graceful legs tangled in his bedsheets while he was parked out here on the sofa— alone. If he let himself kiss her, he'd never survive it.

"Besides…" She brushed past him, toward her over-night bag, propped next to Dillon's school backpack on a nearby chair, as if it belonged there. As if *she* belonged in his house, in his life, in his bed. "Dan said we might not even have to appear in court. He's hoping the suit will never get that far, remember?"

Ryan scrubbed a hand over his face. He remembered, all right. He'd been hyperfocused on every word his lawyer had uttered after Amanda asked him to marry her. It had been the only way he could sit there without obsessing on whatever was going on in her head. He'd just had to push the fact that she'd be going home with him right out of his mind and concentrate on Dan's plan of action.

"I need to ask you something." He looked at her long and hard. A cavernous ache formed deep in his chest when her eyes glittered in response to his stare. "Why are you doing this for me? Tell me the truth."

She could have said any number of things, all of them honorable. All of them kind. But there was only one answer that would render him incapable of turning her down—a few simple words that might bring him to his knees.

"Because you're a good father."

And there it was.

He nodded, throat too clogged with emotion to speak.

"Good night, Ryan." She took a few bashful steps

toward him, then rested her fingertips gently on his shoulder, rose up on tiptoe and pressed a chaste kiss to his cheek.

He stood as still as possible. He didn't trust himself to move a muscle. All it would take was a slight move of his head to the right and he could capture her mouth with his. But if his lips touched hers tonight, it wouldn't end there. Not when he felt as raw and vulnerable as he did just then.

It would have been so damned easy to seek solace in the sweetness of her kiss, in the warm tenderness of her body. Ryan hadn't been with a woman in years. He and Maggie had stopped sleeping together long before her accident. He barely remembered what it was like to have someone want him, *really* want him.

There was something in Amanda's eyes, though— a hot spark of yearning every time she looked at him that reminded him what it meant to be a man. It was like gazing into a mirror and seeing all of his own pent-up desire looking back at him. And he knew…he just *knew*…that if he ever took her to bed, there would be no turning back. He'd never get enough of her. Ever.

They couldn't go there. Not now.

He didn't want to give her his brokenness. If and when he made love to Amanda Sylvester, he wanted to come to her as a whole man. A complete man. A man who could offer her more than what little he had left of his soul to give.

So he squeezed his eyes shut tight and responded in an aching, anguished whisper.

"Good night."

* * *

Ryan, will you marry me?

The words spun round and round in Amanda's head as she turned onto her side in Ryan's bed and buried her face in his pillow. It smelled like him—warm and woodsy. She wanted to breathe it in, as if it could somehow bring her closer to him. Because even though she'd somehow managed to utter those outrageous words, she'd felt like an imposter stretched out on his plush king-size mattress. A fake.

Maybe because that's exactly what you are.

They weren't actually getting married. Of course not. She hadn't even had to spell things out for Ryan when Dan had gotten up from the booth to visit the men's room. He'd lifted his gaze to hers and she'd known with utmost certainty that he hadn't believed her for a minute. He thought she pitied him, that's all. He thought she'd proposed to him out of a desperate move to help him keep custody of his son, which was technically true.

Mostly.

There was more to her feelings for Ryan than mere empathy. She felt so many things for the man that she couldn't begin to identify all her emotions. She only knew that the thought of him losing Dillon made her sick with grief. It couldn't happen. She wouldn't let it.

Dillon worshipped Ryan. Couldn't he see it? Even before they'd adopted Tucker, the little boy's gaze never left his father. In his own quiet way, he'd clung to Ryan. She knew Ryan thought that Tucker had been the one to bring Dillon out of his shell, but she knew better.

Ryan had done the work—all the heavy lifting. Tucker had simply given Dillon the last little push he needed.

She wished she could hate the Brewsters. A hefty dose of rage would probably do her a world of good right now. It definitely would make it easier to forget the sadness she'd seen in Ryan's eyes when she'd kissed him good-night—a sadness so profound, so deep that she wondered if there was any way for him to come back from it.

Try as she might, though, she couldn't muster an ounce of hatred toward Ryan's former in-laws. Sure, they were some of the most horrible and unreasonable people she'd ever come across. But she suspected that the two individuals she'd met at the barbecue cook-off weren't the real Finch and Annabelle. They were what happened to parents when they lost a child in an unexpected, tragic way. They were mired in grief, lashing out at Ryan because he was the easiest target for the pain they wanted so badly to purge.

Couldn't they see what they were doing? If they went through with the lawsuit and somehow ended up tearing Dillon away from Ryan, they would ensure that Ryan suffered the same kind of irreparable loss they'd been living with since the day Maggie died. No parent was ever prepared for the loss of a child.

But Ryan wouldn't lose Dillon. Her spontaneous proposal ensured he wouldn't, and even though there was a small part of her that wished Ryan would have believed it had been genuine, she didn't regret it for a minute. She'd done the right thing, and if she'd had to choose all over again, she'd say the same exact words.

Ryan, will you marry me?

What could possibly go wrong?

Amanda stepped into the Furever Paws lobby the following day for her regular weekly dog walking shift and stopped dead in her tracks.

"Wow." Her gaze flitted from the plastic sheeting covering the floor to the ladders set up around the lobby and finally to Rebekah Taylor sitting behind the counter at the information desk. "You don't waste any time, do you?"

Rebekah grinned. "Thanks to you, we've got the funds to whip this place back into shape. So we may as well get started on the repairs."

"It wasn't just me. The entire town came together to make this happen." Amanda set two paper coffee cups with the Main Street Grille logo printed on them on the counter and slid one toward Rebekah. "It's hazelnut. I thought caffeine might be in order since you're dealing with sawing and hammering all day in addition to a dozen barking dogs and a roomful of nervous cats."

"Well, since you put it that way." Rebekah reached for the coffee and took a long swallow. "Ah, thank you."

Amanda peered toward the hallway at the back of the lobby that led to the kennel area. "Seriously, how are the animals doing with all of this chaos?"

"Pretty good, actually. The dogs aren't the problem." Her cheeks flared pink.

Interesting. Amanda narrowed her gaze. "What exactly is the problem, then?"

"Grant Whitaker." Rebekah pulled a face as if the name left a bad taste in her mouth. "Sorry, I know he's Birdie and Bunny's nephew and he seems to care for them a great deal, but the man is driving me insane."

"He's still here? I thought he only came up from Florida for the weekend to help out at the barbecue. Shouldn't he be back in Jacksonville by now?"

"He postponed his trip for a few days so he could spy on me," Rebekah said primly.

Amanda laughed. "Come on. That can't be true."

"No, really. I don't think he trusts me. He's like a dog who thinks I've come onto his territory to steal all his bones. I don't have any idea what I did to give him the impression that I might take advantage of his aunts. I'm here because I love animals and want to help them." Rebekah took another sip of her coffee and Amanda noticed her earrings were shaped like little paw prints.

"I'm sure he realizes that. The sisters are certainly glad you're here. When I talked to Birdie and Bunny after the cook-off on Saturday they had nothing but great things to say about you." They'd also waxed poetic about Doc J, but that was nothing new. "Don't worry about Grant. Like you said, he's leaving soon anyway."

"But he'll be back again before long. He wants to help with the rebuilding."

That was probably for the best, considering Gator had dropped the ball on the insurance. Maybe Grant wanted to keep a closer eye on things to make sure nothing else was amiss with the business end of things.

But Amanda wasn't about to share the Whitakers' personal family business with Rebekah, no matter how much she liked her. She had a feeling they might end up as friends—*actual* friends, as opposed to whatever she and Ryan were at the moment.

"If Grant will be spending more time in Spring Forest, I'm sure you two will eventually learn to like each other." Amanda winked. "He's really not that bad. I promise."

"I believe you. You brought me delicious hazelnut coffee, so I'm sure you're trustworthy."

"Maybe you should try that with Grant since he seems skeptical about you. Just a thought," Amanda said, only half joking. Who didn't love hazelnut?

Rebekah laughed, then switched her attention to the ringing telephone. "Furever Paws."

Amanda made her way to the kennel area, marveling at the fact that the repairs to the roof were already underway. A few of the other local businesses that had sustained damage in the storm had also begun construction.

After the tornado whirled through town, she'd kept thinking about the twister in the movie *The Wizard of Oz* and how it transported Dorothy and Toto to a magical new land over the rainbow where daring adventures awaited them. Everything was more vivid and colorful than it had been before.

Sometimes she felt like that's what had happened to

her and Tucker when the storm hit Spring Forest. Overnight, everything changed. At first, it had been terrifying, but maybe she just hadn't realized how much she'd needed her life to be spun around and infused with color. Since the tornado struck, she'd helped Tucker get out of the shelter once and for all. She'd put together a fundraiser that had brought people together from all over the state for a common purpose. In a way, she'd finally moved past the Sadie Hawkins incident. If she could fake-propose to a man without getting sick to her stomach, she might eventually end up in a real romantic relationship.

She liked the way her life had changed, and as much as she wanted Furever Paws to put itself back together, it suddenly felt as if time was spinning backward. Everything was slowly but surely returning to normal. Unlike Dorothy, Amanda wasn't trying to get back to the way things had been before. She didn't want to go home—not if it meant giving up everything she'd discovered in the wake of the tornado.

Especially Ryan and Dillon.

But some things were too good to be true. Intellectually, she knew that, just as she knew that Ryan wasn't really her fiancé. They were pretending for the sake of the lawsuit. They'd simply told Dillon she was staying over for a few days because her apartment was being painted. The little boy had been through enough turmoil—he didn't need to be dragged into their faux romance unless it became absolutely necessary. She'd cooked them breakfast this morning and kissed Dillon's soft little cheek when he'd left for school, but they weren't her family and eventually she'd have to go home.

Just like Dorothy, because in the end even Oz turned out to be nothing but a dream.

Chapter Thirteen

It was the little things about sharing his home with Amanda that got to Ryan the most—the unexpected things, the bittersweet surprises that made him realize how easy it would be to blend their separate lives into one.

He learned to brace himself for the irresistible sight of her in her cute little pajamas in the mornings, just as he knew better than to linger too long when she kissed him good-night. It was never more than an innocent peck, just like the one she'd given him on the very first night. But somehow those chaste kisses sharpened his hunger for her even more fiercely than if she'd given him a full openmouthed kiss.

So he knew to simply hold his breath and concentrate all his energy into not touching her until it was over and the moment had passed. It never got any easier, though. If anything, it took longer and longer for his inevitable erection to recede as those first few days turned into a full week of living together.

But again, the moments that caught him off guard were the ones that ended up feeling as if they'd grabbed him by the throat and refused to let go—like the first time he'd opened the door to his closet and seen her soft jeans and flirty little dresses hanging side by side next to his tailored suits and starched oxford shirts. Or the time they'd shared the bathroom sink and brushed their teeth together, locking gazes in the mirror. And the night Dillon had woken up in tears, shaken by a nightmare, and Ryan had found Amanda curled beside him in his tiny twin bed the next morning.

Those were the little intimacies that strung together like pearls on a string, one after another, eventually building a life. A home. A family.

How could he have forgotten? He'd been married for most of his adult life. But it had been such a long time since he'd felt any real connection to Maggie that he'd grown accustomed to a solitary existence. For the last few years of their marriage, they'd merely coexisted.

But now…

Now he'd been plunged into a world of spun sugar domestic bliss, all wrapped up and tied with a ribbon of barely contained desire. And he liked it, damn it. He liked it far more than he should have.

"Mr. Carter, shall I lock up or will you be working late?" Jonah lingered in the doorway of Ryan's office with his messenger bag slung over his shoulder.

Ryan glanced at the time display in the upper right-hand corner of his computer screen. It was nearly six o'clock, hardly late compared to the hours he'd kept when he worked at the *Post*. But he wasn't in DC anymore. He was in Spring Forest, and he didn't want to be sitting behind a desk at the paper when his son had already been done school for hours.

Then why are you here?

Because he was hiding, that's why. He was avoiding the cozy scene at home before it broke him. He wasn't ready for another relationship, and even though the one he had with Amanda was only a charade, it was beginning to feel more real than anything he'd had in a long, long time. She picked Dillon up from school and cooked their meals. She didn't have to do those things, but she did.

Ryan pushed his chair away from his desk and stood. "I'll walk out with you, Jonah."

Falling back into old habits and pouring himself into his work wasn't the answer. He knew that. Plus Dillon was having his first official playdate tonight. The Sutton girls had invited him over for pizza and ice cream. Ryan wanted to be home when Dan came to pick him up in case Dillon got nervous and changed his mind about going.

"After you, sir." Jonah gestured for Ryan to step in front of him.

Sir again. He gave the young man a withering stare.

Jonah cleared his throat. "I mean…um…let's go. Um, Ryan."

"Better." He laughed and clapped Jonah on the back. "We'll get there."

He pulled his car onto the sun-dappled streets of Kingdom Creek with a half hour to spare before Dillon left for the Suttons' house. Amanda was taking advantage of her brother-in-law Paul's extended time at the Grille and had come home early, excited to teach Dillon how to make some kid-friendly hors d'oeuvres to take with him on his playdate. Last night she'd mapped out an elaborate plan that included sausage sticks and bread dough arranged to look like little sleeping dogs. Ryan had done a double take when he'd seen how closely they resembled Tucker.

But when he turned the SUV into the driveway, he found Amanda and Dillon in the front yard instead of the kitchen. Tucker was there too, looking grumpier than Ryan had ever seen him before, sitting in a tub full of soapsuds while Dillon patted him down with a giant yellow sponge.

Ryan sat behind the wheel for a minute, fighting the pang in his chest as he took in the sight. It was straight out of a Hallmark movie—the kind where nothing bad ever happens. Where there were no car accidents or custody hearings. Where kids could just be kids and adults could love one another, free of complication.

The very best sort of make-believe.

He climbed out of the car, loosening his tie as he joined the sentimental scene. God help him, nothing about the easy grin on Dillon's face or the way his heart skittered to a stop at the sight of Amanda's curves in

her damp clothes felt like an act. Was he still pretending? Had he *ever* been just putting on an act?

"What's this?" He forced a laugh, but his voice be-
trayed him. The ache in his words echoed the one in
his heart.

Amanda stood, peeling back a wet strand of hair
from her face. "Tucker rolled in something in the backyard, and Dillon's snacks are all packed up and ready to
go, so we figured we'd give your naughty dog a bath."

"My naughty dog?" He shoved his hands in his
pockets to keep himself from wrapping his arms
around her waist and pulling her beautiful wet body
up against his.

"So naughty," Dillon said. "Daddy, he smelled so
bad."

Daddy. Ryan cleared his throat. "I guess it's a good
thing you got him all cleaned up, then."

"Dan's here early." Amanda looked past Ryan and
waved.

Dan's car slowed to a stop at the curb.

"Dillon, why don't you run inside and dry off. Don't
forget the snacks you and Amanda made." Ryan handed
him one of the striped bath towels from the heap piled
on the lawn a few feet away from the tub of soapy
water.

Dillon obeyed, walking to the house with a spring
in his step and a waterlogged, cantankerous Tucker
sloshing behind him.

"Oh no." Amanda stifled a laugh. "Maybe I should
go grab the dog."

"It's okay." Ryan winked at her. "What's a little water on the floor?"

"You two sure look cozy," Dan said as he crossed the lawn.

Ryan glanced at Amanda, and the blood seemed to pump faster through his veins as he registered the flush that crept across her face.

"You know…" Dan's gaze narrowed as he studied them. "I had my doubts about the spontaneous marriage proposal, especially after you both asked me to keep the engagement a secret. But I trust my clients, and if you tell me you're engaged, that means you're engaged. Now I can see it, though."

"What do you mean?" Amanda bit her bottom lip.

She did that sometimes when she was nervous. Ryan had picked up on that little tell over the past few days.

"I mean, look at you. Anyone driving down the street could tell that you're crazy about each other. It's written all over your faces." He shrugged. "I'm happy for you, that's all. Maybe you can squeeze in a date night while Dillon is over at our house tonight."

"Date night." Amanda's gaze flitted toward Ryan, lingering ever so briefly on his mouth. "That sounds fun."

Indeed it does.

"The girls are excited. I should probably get Dillon back there pretty quick before they start blowing up my phone. They're supposed to be straightening their rooms, but when I left just now, our housekeeper seemed to be doing most of the heavy lifting." Dan waved at Dillon as he climbed down the porch steps carrying a flat Tupperware container. "You ready, little dude?"

Dillon nodded, and after giving Ryan a quick one-armed hug, he followed Dan to his car. Just as he was about to climb inside, he hesitated and looked over his shoulder.

"Uh-oh." Ryan's jaw clenched.

Amanda frowned. "Do you think he's changing his mind? He seemed thrilled earlier."

Dillon ran back toward them, but he still had that easy smile on his face. Ryan figured he must have forgotten something—his dinosaur maybe.

But no, that wasn't it at all.

He threw his arms around Amanda's legs and grinned up at her. "I forgot to tell you goodbye."

Then he was off again, darting back to Dan's car.

Amanda stood dripping just inside Ryan's foyer, struggling to catch her breath.

Dillon's embrace had caught her off guard, but it wasn't the sweetness of his actions that had knocked the wind out of her. It was what he'd said.

I forgot to tell you goodbye.

She squeezed her eyes closed and tried to push the words out her head, but she couldn't. Now that they'd been let loose, they kept repeating on an unending loop in her mind, always in Dillon's quiet little sing-song voice.

Goodbye.

Goodbye.

Goodbye.

"You okay?" Ryan's gaze traveled over her, leaving a rush of goose bumps in its wake.

She wrapped her arms around herself and nodded. "Fine."

Not fine. *So* not fine. When she'd thrown her hat in the ring as Ryan's fake fiancé, she'd been so eager to help Ryan and Dillon stay together that she hadn't given any thought to what their temporary arrangement would do to Ryan's son once it ended.

He'd lost his mom. There was still a chance he could lose Ryan. And now she'd inserted herself into his life, knowing all the while that he'd lose her too. When the custody battle was over, she was going to pack up her things and walk out the door. How could she possibly explain it to him? How could he understand when he couldn't even go on a playdate without making sure he told her goodbye first?

"Come on, I know you're freezing." Ryan held up a towel, arched a brow and waited for her to step into it.

She hesitated. She felt too raw all of a sudden to play house—maybe because Dillon's tender goodbye had rattled her or maybe because for the very first time in their faux engagement, she and Ryan were alone in the house together.

Probably both.

Whatever the reason, she wasn't sure she could stand that close to him in his little hushed cottage and not take their game of pretend one step too far. But at the same time, there was a challenge in his gaze as he peered at her over the top of the towel. If she didn't know better, she would've thought he was daring her to come nearer.

Maybe he actually was.

Challenge accepted.

If Ryan wasn't fazed by the sudden intimacy of their situation, then neither was she. She was tired of being weak, tired of waiting for things to happen to her instead of making them happen all on her own. If the tornado and its aftermath had taught her anything, it was that she was stronger than she thought she was.

She squared her shoulders and stepped into Ryan's outstretched arms, holding her breath as she waited for him to release the towel. But he didn't—not at first, anyway. Instead he wrapped the plush terry cloth around her trembling form and then gingerly...slowly... *achingly* slowly...he began patting her dry.

He spent whole minutes on her legs alone, running the soft towel over her calves and then higher, mercifully ignoring the shiver that coursed through her when his hand brushed against the inside of her thighs. Then he moved to her arms and shoulders, and his face was mere inches away. He concentrated so thoroughly on his task that he never quite met her gaze, but that was okay because it left her free to study his features up close—his lips, his nose, his chiseled jaw. His eyelashes, dark as soot.

He was the most beautiful man she'd ever seen, and no matter what happened between them after Dillon's custody was secure and they went their separate ways, that would always be the case. He was the standard by which all the other men in her life would be measured. He was the one.

She audibly swallowed, and the corner of his lips hitched up just a tiny fraction of an inch. If she hadn't been staring at his mouth, mesmerized, she would have missed it entirely.

He wasn't *The One*, as in capitalized letters and something borrowed and something blue. He couldn't be. Amanda hadn't been looking for The One. She'd just been minding her own business, dreaming up recipes people would never eat and biding her time at the Grille. As Belle always said, she'd practically been hiding.

And he found you anyway.

She took a shuddering inhale. This was getting weird. She wasn't a child. She was perfectly capable of drying herself off.

But even as her mind told her to snatch the towel away from him and finish the job herself, her eyes drifted closed as he walked behind her and she tipped her head back, letting him gather her slippery wet hair in his hands.

He was close enough for Amanda to feel his warm breath on the back of her neck. She could even smell the lingering traces of his familiar aftershave, and oddly enough, that was what finally did her in. She'd fallen asleep wrapped in that masculine scent for the past several nights, dreaming of a frosted pine forest as his bedsheets tangled around her legs. That scent did things to her. Things that frightened and fascinated her in equal parts.

"I know what you're doing," she whispered.

He stroked her hair with the towel for several long seconds until he finally responded. "Do you?"

She longed to peer over her shoulder. The fact that she could feel him, smell him and hear every sultry intake of his breath but she could no longer see him was maddening. She would have been lying if she said she didn't like it, though. She liked it quite a lot. She was enjoying everything about this strange, quiet seduction...

If, in fact, that's what it was.

It had to be, though. Didn't it?

She squeezed her eyes shut tight and went ahead and said it. "You're trying to seduce me."

"I'm pampering you. I had a feeling you wouldn't recognize the experience." He inched closer until she felt the hard press of his erection against her backside. A whimper escaped her, and the towel fell from Ryan's hands to the floor, where it pooled around their feet. "Tell me—when was the last time someone took care of *you*?"

Her eyes swam with hot tears. She gave her head a nearly imperceptible shake.

Never.

There hadn't been a last time. No one had ever taken care of her before. Not like this. She'd always been the one who'd done the nurturing, the one who'd done more...the one who'd *cared* more. And now Ryan was showing her what it felt like to be treasured, to be adored.

I can't.

It was too overwhelming, maybe because she felt

like Dillon's goodbye was still wrapped around her heart, squeezing it tight. Or maybe because being pampered felt far too much like being loved. It didn't really matter why. She just knew that if she didn't walk away right now, she never would. And yet her feet just wouldn't move.

Ryan swept her hair to one side, over her shoulder. Then he touched the side of her neck with a featherlight brush of his fingertips. "I want to kiss you in this exact spot." His voice was a low growl that she felt deep in her center. Velvety smooth. "I've wanted to kiss you here for days. May I?"

She bit down hard on her lip, but it was no use.

"Yes, please," she murmured.

She sounded desperate. Needy. But when his lips made contact with the curve of her neck, she didn't care how she sounded. She didn't care what would happen tomorrow or the next day or the day after that.

She wanted to be Dorothy in Oz for just a little while longer…as long as she could.

She took a deep breath and turned to face him. There were questions in his eyes—questions he didn't need to ask because she whispered *yes* again. Yes to it all. Yes to everything.

And when his mouth came down on hers, it felt like he was kissing away the goodbyes that frightened her so. Because a kiss this pure, this passionate could only be one thing. Not an ending and not a goodbye, but a prelude. A searing-hot promise of things to come.

Her pulse roared in her ears and she ran her hands over Ryan's chest—touching, exploring—letting them do all the things she'd been dying to do since the day he'd first stalked into her restaurant ordering drinks they didn't serve. He'd seemed so out of place back then, as if the tornado had picked him up in Washington and deposited him in Spring Forest just for her.

But he fit here now, just like his hardness fit perfectly against her grasp when she let her hands drift lower. And lower still.

He groaned into her mouth and a shudder coursed through her.

There's no place like home.

Chapter Fourteen

Ryan wasn't sure how long he and Amanda stood just inside the door, kissing and touching and exploring. Hours, perhaps? Days? Time seemed to come to a standstill and in between the sighs and the quickened breaths, his mind could only snag on one conscious thought—*finally.*

They'd been barreling toward this moment for so long, but every time they'd come close to making any sort of real connection with each other, something got in the way. At least that's what he'd thought. He'd been wrong, though. He realized that now. As much as he wanted to take her to bed, as much as he *needed* to feel her softness surrounding him as he pushed inside her, making love to her wouldn't be the act that bonded them together. Their hearts and souls were already intertwined. While they'd been pretending to be a couple, something very real had taken place—they'd slipped into intimacy.

All Ryan's life, he'd thought intimacy was the kind of thing that required pursuit. Intention. People didn't just accidentally develop feelings for one another without noticing.

Except maybe they did.

No.

It was his lust talking. How was he supposed to think straight when he'd been celibate for so long? Of course he was confusing physical intimacy with real, soul-deep connection. His body was surging with testosterone, let loose after years of being pent up. They'd been *pretending*, for crying out loud. It was all an act. None of it was real.

Why did he keep forgetting that important detail?

He adjusted the angle of his head so he could kiss Amanda more deeply, more thoroughly. She made a tiny mewing sound he loved so much, soft like a kitten, and Ryan couldn't think anymore. About anything. He could only give and take and feel, and for once in his long, lonely life, he was fine with that. He and Amanda would figure things out in the morning. They only had a few hours together before Dan was scheduled to bring Dillon home, and Ryan wanted to make the most of every damned minute.

Date night.

The words rang in his mind like a bell, tricking him into wondering if this is what life would be like if they made their temporary arrangement permanent.

Between the playdates and the school runs, would they always have *this*? He couldn't fathom a relationship any more different than the one he'd had with Maggie. He'd blamed himself for the disconnect between the two of them. He'd been the one to seek solace in his office. He'd been the bad person in the marriage, the broken one.

When Amanda looked at him—when she touched him the way she was stroking him now—he no longer felt that way. For the first time in years, he felt whole.

What was happening? Sex wasn't supposed to be this way. Sex was just…sex. This felt like so much more, and they hadn't even undressed yet. Amanda's damp clothes still clung to her curves, and somehow he could see everything and nothing all at the same time. Her body was exquisite—shapely and lithe, but he wanted to know more. Needed it.

He wanted to know how she liked to be touched. He wanted to know what it felt like to slide inside her. Most of all, he wanted to see the look in her eyes when she finally let go and came apart.

He let out an aching breath and pulled back to study her expression. The sight of her swollen mouth and darkened irises made him groan again.

"So lovely," he whispered. "You're the most beautiful woman I've ever known."

She smiled, and he dragged the pad of his thumb against the delicious swell of her bottom lip before kissing her again. How did she taste so good? He'd lain awake on his sofa for hours the past few nights just thinking about that taste.

His hands fisted in her hair, and he moved his mouth to her ear. "Tell me you want me."

He needed to hear her say it before they went any further. He needed to know they were in this together, and it wasn't just him out there all alone, blinded by desire.

She rose up on tiptoe and nipped at his earlobe. "I want you, Ryan. So, so much. More than I've ever wanted anyone before."

His erection swelled almost to the point of pain. Then he heard a zipper coming undone and still didn't realize Amanda had opened his fly until her hand slipped inside his pants and her warm hand closed around his shaft.

Oh my God.

He took a sharp inhale.

"Don't move," he whispered between gasps. "*Please* don't move."

She peered up at him and that look, coupled with the softness of her breasts against his chest, was nearly enough to make him come. *No.* He needed it to last as long as possible. Weeks, months, years.

Maybe even forever.

He reached for her wrist, removing her hand from his body and weaving her fingers though his. Then he led her to his bed, where she'd been sleeping alone for the past seven nights, and he peeled the damp clothes from her body, one piece at a time, worshipping her soft brown skin as he went.

When at last she stretched out naked before him, he stepped out of his clothes and let her touch him again.

He tried not to think about how perfect she looked, gazing up at him as she reached for him and guided him to her entrance. But it was no use. When he pushed inside her radiant body, which inexplicably seemed as familiar as it did brand-new, he was struck with the profound realization that she belonged there—not just in his bed, but in his life.

In his family.

He began to move, sliding in and out at an excruciatingly languid pace, marveling at the beautiful woman beneath him. He wished he could tell her that whatever happened after tonight, everything would be okay. He wished he could beg her to stay and swear to her that she'd never live alone again because he'd always be there to take care of her, to pamper her, even when she insisted on putting everyone else's needs ahead of her own.

But he couldn't say those things to her—not even now—so he kissed her instead, swallowing her aching cries.

He didn't deserve her. Not even temporarily. That was a fact. And in the end, that's how he knew whatever they had couldn't possibly be real.

No matter how badly he wanted to believe otherwise.

Amanda woke to the smell of bacon wafting toward Ryan's bedroom from the kitchen. She took a deep, luscious inhale before opening her eyes.

God, she loved bacon.

Didn't everyone? That's why the Grille went through

fifty pounds of it a week. Back when Amanda's parents managed the Grille, she used to cook the bacon during the breakfast shift on the weekends. She'd line up the strips in neat rows, enough to cover the surface of the entire grill from end to end.

But never in her life had anyone cooked bacon just for her.

She threw off the covers and climbed out of bed, anxious to see what was happening down the hall in Ryan's quaint kitchen. Especially if whatever it was involved Ryan himself. Her need to see him again was visceral. They'd made love twice before Dan dropped Dillon off at home. When the doorbell rang, Ryan dragged himself out of bed, gave her one last kiss and said he'd see her in the morning.

They'd actually had a date night of sorts, just as Dan had suggested.

The only way it could have been better was if Ryan had come back to bed after he'd read Dillon his bedtime story, tucked him in and made sure Tucker was situated in his place of honor at the foot of Dillon's bed. But it made sense for him to stay on the sofa. Amanda was only in the house so that the engagement would look real for the court.

They'd never discussed what would happen if their romance suddenly became real.

Don't get ahead of yourself.

Amanda slipped into her bathrobe and tightened the sash into a knot a little too forcefully.

She didn't know what last night had meant, and that

was okay. She didn't need to know. Not yet. Not while they still had time.

They'd figure things out once the lawsuit was over, and according to Dan, a custody battle like the one Ryan was facing could take anywhere from three weeks to six months. In the meantime, she and Ryan would have to keep playing house.

Amanda's hands shook as she twisted her hair into a messy bun. Playing house had seemed much less dangerous when her heart wasn't part of the game.

But she was overthinking things again. Hadn't she decided she was going to take more chances? What had happened to her big tornado-induced awakening? Ryan, Dillon and Tucker were all right down the hall. She still had one foot planted squarely in Oz, and to her complete and utter delight, Oz had bacon.

When she padded into the kitchen, she found Ryan standing at the sink in a T-shirt and running shorts, washing a frying pan. Dillon sat at the kitchen table, munching on a strip of bacon and drawing pictures with his crayons while Tucker gazed hopefully up at him from the floor. Amanda did a double take when she saw the spread of food. The platter in the center of the table was piled high with biscuits. Granted, they were a little misshapen, but they definitely looked home-made. An assortment of jams and jellies surrounded the platter, and beside it, she spotted a plate of bacon. It all looked so homey, so…perfect.

For some silly reason, she almost felt like crying.

"Good morning," Ryan said, winking at her as he ran a dish towel over the frying pan and placed it in one of the cabinets. He gestured at the table with a flourish. "Surprise!"

She swallowed around the knot in her throat. "You made me breakfast?"

"I helped," Dillon chimed in.

"You sure did, bud." Then, solemnly, Ryan added, "Dillon was on biscuit duty."

Amanda smiled. "I don't know what to say. No one's made breakfast for me in years."

Ryan's expression grew tender. Serious. And suddenly he was looking at her just like he had the night before when he'd so carefully toweled her dry.

I'm pampering you.

He was saying it to her again, only with his eyes this time, and for a brief, shining moment, she believed Oz might not be just a dream, after all. It was beginning to feel more and more like home every day.

But then Ryan's cell blared to life. It vibrated its way across the kitchen counter, breaking the mood's magic spell with its jarring ringtone.

He glanced at the display. "I'd better take this. It's Dan."

"Of course. I'll just keep myself busy with the giant plate of bacon over there."

He picked up the phone but before he answered it, he gave the sash of her robe a playful tug and kissed her gently on the mouth. "Hello?"

Amanda took a seat beside Dillon and plucked a strip of bacon from the plate on the table.

"What?" Ryan grew still, and Amanda knew at once

that the call must be related to the custody case, but she couldn't tell whether the news was good or bad.

"I see." He nodded and began to pace the length of the cozy kitchen. Back and forth, back and forth. "So what would that entail, exactly?"

Amanda searched his gaze, and at last he smiled.

"Right. We can talk about that later. I'll be in the office most of the day. Give me a call anytime. And, ah, Dan…" Ryan took a deep inhale, and for a second he looked like he might break down and weep. "Thank you…thank you so much."

He pressed the end-call button and stared at the phone for a long moment, as if trying to wrap his mind around what had just transpired. When he finally glanced up, his smile was so broad that he looked like the weight of the world had just been lifted off his shoulders.

"The Brewsters have withdrawn the lawsuit. It's over."

Chapter Fifteen

"I can't believe it." Amanda's head spun. She felt like she might faint. "I didn't see this coming at all. Did you?"

Ryan raked a hand through his hair and blew out a breath. "No. Not in a million years. I'm thrilled, obviously. I think I'm just in a state of shock right now. I can't believe it's over."

Over.

Amanda knew he was talking about the lawsuit, not about them. Of course she knew that. But every time he used that word, she felt a little pang in her heart. She just couldn't help it.

"Dillon, bud," Ryan rested a gentle hand on Dillon's shoulder. Looking at them together made the lump in Amanda's throat double in size. Dillon belonged with

Ryan. He always had. "We have to leave for school soon. Can you go brush your teeth and get your backpack together?"

Dillon obediently climbed down from his chair and headed to the bathroom. Tucker cast a wistful glance in the general direction of the bacon, scrunched his furry brow in frustration and then trotted after the little boy.

Amanda lowered her voice to a whisper. "Now that Dillon's gone, can you elaborate? The suspense is killing me. Did Dan say why Maggie's parents changed their minds?"

"Apparently, they were never all that serious about wanting custody to begin with." Ryan shook his head. "Can you believe it?"

"No, that's awful. Why would they put you and Dillon through such a thing if they never really wanted him to live with them?"

"Dan had a long talk with their attorney in DC early this morning and she finally admitted that what the Brewsters really want is more time with Dillon. They're upset they can't see him as often as they did before we moved to Spring Forest. All this time, the custody suit has been nothing but a bargaining chip. Now that they've withdrawn the paperwork, Finch and Annabelle are hoping I'll be amenable to scheduling regular trips for Dillon to go to DC."

"How do you feel about that?" Amanda said.

Ryan took a deep breath. "Okay, I guess. My intention was never to keep Dillon away from his grandparents permanently. We just needed some space. I wanted to get to know my son and I couldn't do that with them constantly breathing down my neck. Plus one of my old college professors ran the newspaper here, and he was ready to retire. He'd been my mentor for years and when he heard I was looking to get out of Washington, he offered to turn *The Spring Forest Chronicle* over to me. It seemed like fate."

Their eyes met for a moment, and then he looked away.

"Dan is going to give me a call later so we can choose a date for Dillon's first visit." Ryan glanced at the time on his iPhone.

"If you need to get going, I can clean up the breakfast dishes."

He shook his head. "No, no. I can't have you cleaning up this mess. That would defeat the whole purpose of making you breakfast. Besides, you've done so much for us already. I'm sure you're relieved I won't have to rely on you so much anymore."

She stared at him. *Relieved?* Was that seriously how he thought she felt? "I wanted to help you and Dillon. I have all along, since before the lawsuit even happened."

"Sure, of course. I know that. I just meant…"

"What, exactly?" Amanda's voice came out sharper than she'd intended, but a tight knot of panic had suddenly lodged itself in her chest and she was having trouble articulating exactly how she felt.

Probably because what she felt scared her to death.

I love him. I love them both.

Oh God, she did.

She was in love with Ryan. She'd been in love with him from the very start. Birdie and Mollie had been right all along—she had a weak spot for grumpy males, both dogs and humans alike.

No. She shook her head. She didn't want to be in love with Ryan Carter, especially not when he was acting so strange, as if they hadn't shared a bed last night.

Ryan sighed. "All I'm trying to say is that now that the lawsuit is over…"

She held up a hand to cut him off. "Would you *please* stop saying that word?"

He reared back as if she'd slapped him. "What word?"

"Over." Her voice broke and to her complete and utter mortification, her face crumpled. Hot, humiliating tears streamed down her face.

"Don't cry, love. Please don't cry. Talk to me. I don't understand why you're so upset." He moved to brush a tear from her cheek, and she leaned out of his reach.

She didn't want him to touch her. Not now. If he did, she'd fall apart even worse than she already had. She was in this alone, wasn't she?

He wasn't in love with her.

If he were, he wouldn't be acting as if they'd both just gotten a get-out-of-jail-free card now that they would no longer have to "pretend" to be in love.

I'm sure you're relieved I won't have to rely on you so much anymore.

She stood, and the chair she'd been sitting in clattered to the floor. "I'm sorry, Ryan. I think I should go."

Ever so slowly, he righted the chair. Maybe he was just trying to calm her down and defuse the situation, but his movements were so careful and deliberate that they reminded her of the gentle way he'd dried her off yesterday. And the reverence in his fingertips when he'd raised the hem of her sodden T-shirt and lifted it tenderly over her head.

She didn't want to think about those things right now. They hurt too much. She'd been wrong to believe she could stay in Oz when she didn't truly belong there. She never had. Now she just wanted everything to go back to the way it was before—to a time when she could simply admire Ryan from afar without knowing what it felt like to have him move inside her or kiss her with a hunger she'd never experienced before.

But she couldn't go back. It was too late.

He reached for the sash of her robe again and used it to pull her closer toward him, to reel her back in. Her rebellious heart skipped a beat.

This was it—the moment of truth. He didn't have to come out and tell her he loved her. She couldn't bring herself to say it, so it was okay if he couldn't either. All he had to say was one word...one tiny syllable.

Stay.

He cleared his throat, and that split second of hesitation was all the indication she needed. She knew. She just *knew*. He wasn't going to say it. He was going to let her walk right out the door.

"Daddy."

Dillon entered the kitchen once again, with his backpack slung over one shoulder and Tucker nestled in his arms. Amanda's bottom lip quivered so hard that she had to bite it and look away.

"I'm ready. I brushed my teeth just like you asked me to," Dillon said.

"I need to get him to school," Ryan said quietly. Then he grabbed his keys from the bowl on the kitchen counter where he always kept them, and without so much as a backward glance, he walked past her toward the foyer.

"Come on, bud. Let's go." He stood waiting for Dillon to catch up.

And for a second or two, Amanda was able to hold herself together. She'd already made enough of a scene. She just wanted to wait until Ryan and Dillon left. Then she could gather her things and head back to her own apartment, where she could fall apart in private.

But then she felt Dillon's arms wrap around her legs from behind, holding her tight. And it was too much. Much more than she could take. Her heart felt like it was being ripped right out of her chest.

And then in his gentle, little boy voice, he said, "Goodbye, Amanda."

Ryan had messed up.

He'd messed things up in a major way.

Amanda had been waiting for him to say something, and he'd done what he always did when things got too personal—he'd bolted.

He went through the motions at the office, filing stories and approving the layouts for the week's edition of the paper. He talked to Dan and worked out a proposed schedule for Dillon to visit his grandparents at regular intervals. But while his head was at work and tied up with thoughts of the new visitation schedule, his heart was back in the kitchen, watching the tears stream down Amanda's face as she waited for him to acknowledge what had happened between them the night before.

Instead, he'd walked away.

How could he have been such an idiot?

He'd told himself he was doing it for her. He'd made a mess of every personal relationship he'd ever had, and he didn't want to repeat the same old mistakes with her. She was too precious to get her heart broken like that. She was too damned special.

But he'd broken her heart anyway by refusing to admit what he'd suspected for a while now—he loved her. *Of course* he loved her. He just hadn't wanted to admit it because even though he'd been trying his level best to change, to become a better man, he knew he couldn't take it if Amanda ever looked at him the way Maggie had during the final years of their marriage. After all, there were no guarantees. He'd failed before, and he could very well fail again. This morning had been proof positive that he was capable of letting someone down...even someone he loved.

He turned off his computer and pushed away from his desk. He didn't know what to do with regards to Amanda, but he knew one thing for certain—the office was the last place he should be right now.

"I'll be out for the rest of the day," he said to Jonah, who'd turned up this morning in an actual suit instead of his customary hipster ensemble.

On any other occasion, Ryan would have rejoiced

at the change in his assistant's appearance. But today, the sight of that suit made him feel like the world's biggest jerk. Jonah was clearly trying to emulate him. He'd probably been saving up for weeks to buy a suit like the ones Ryan usually wore to the office. Ryan knew what kind of money Jonah made, and it wasn't much.

He didn't deserve that kind of admiration. He didn't devote an entire afternoon a week to walking homeless dogs at Furever Paws. He'd never even done that once. Nor had he spent whole days organizing a fundraiser so the shelter would have a roof over its head. He'd also never moved in with someone he barely knew in order to help them at a time when they needed it most.

Amanda had done those things, because she was the kind of person who deserved to be emulated, to be loved and adored.

"Shall I forward your calls to your cell?" Jonah asked.

"No." Ryan shook his head. "I'm sure you can deal with any crises around here. I trust you."

Jonan blinked, stunned. "Thank you, sir. Thank you so much."

Ryan nodded, and didn't bother telling him again to drop the *sir*. He was about ready to declare that a losing battle.

When he left the building, the urge to stop by the Grille was almost overwhelming. But he wasn't ready. He had no clue what he could possibly say to make up for all the things that had gone wrong this morning, and he wasn't altogether sure he should try. The hardest part was over. He'd walked away, and maybe now the right thing to do was to *stay* away.

He wished he knew for certain what the right thing was to do. What he wanted most of all was a sign— some small glimmer of confirmation that he could do right by her and they were indeed meant to be together. But Ryan knew better than to believe in that kind of thing. Real life was messy and uncertain, and he and Amanda didn't exist in a vacuum. Ryan had to think about Dillon's needs too.

But in the end, his fragile son was the one who gave him the sign he'd wished for.

When Ryan got home and walked into the kitchen, Dillon's crayons were still scattered over the table and the drawing he'd been working on during breakfast was sitting right there, front and center. Ryan would have known that stick figure anywhere. It was Amanda, carefully rendered by Dillon's tiny hand. He'd drawn her picture more than once in recent days. One of his Crayola portraits of her was tacked onto the refrigerator door with a magnet.

The pictures Dillon drew of Amanda varied—sometimes she was cooking and other times the drawing showed her walking a dog—but there was always one noticeable constant. Dillon spelled out her name in red letters across the top of the page. All caps. *A-M-A-N-D-A.*

And that's where the drawing from this morning differed.

The stick figure resembled all his other depictions of Amanda, and to eliminate any doubt, he'd shown her working at the Grille, standing behind the counter with a big smiley-face-style grin. But he hadn't written her name across the top of the page. Instead, he'd spelled out something else—five precious letters.

M-O-M-M-Y.

"Hello, sugar." Birdie greeted Amanda with a kiss on the cheek and then planted a hand on her hip and frowned. "Wait a minute. What are you doing here at the shelter? This isn't your regular shift."

"Nope, it's not." Amanda shook her head. "But I'm making some changes. I should have more free time on my hands than I've had for the past few years, so you'll probably be seeing more of me around here."

She glanced around at the surrounding dog kennels, all of them full. Most of the pups were new just since last week. As the dogs at the shelter got adopted out and placed in forever homes, new ones came in and took their place. Tucker's old kennel had already provided temporary shelter to three different dogs since he'd gone home with Ryan and Dillon.

It was a never-ending cycle, which was precisely why Amanda kept coming back. Week after week, month after month, year after year. The more time she devoted to helping dogs get socialized, the more likely they were to get adopted. More adoptions meant more space for other strays or unwanted animals. Furever Paws Animal Rescue was just that—a rescue. They were in the business of saving lives. Amanda had seen it happen, time and time again. Sometimes the animals were the ones who ended up getting rescued. More often than not, though, the pets were the ones who ended up doing the saving, just like Tucker saved Dillon.

"I don't understand." Birdie picked up a nearby broom and began sweeping the concrete floor. The dogs in the kennels all swiveled their heads to and fro, following the swish-swish motion of the broom. "I love having you here. You know I do. But if you're walking dogs, who's running the Main Street Grille?"

Amanda smiled. "My brother-in-law, Paul. He's been doing such a great job that I asked him if he wanted to take over as manager and he said yes. He's been unhappy at his office job for quite a while, and he's really loved working at the Grille. It's a win-win for us both. I've decided to start my own catering company."

"That's wonderful, dear! I'm so happy for you. You'll be great at that."

"I hope so." Amanda took a deep breath. "My parents were really surprised when I told them, but they're actually excited for me. Especially now that Paul wants to keep running the Grille. It will remain in our family, just like always."

She was still a little scared to finally take a chance on the dream she'd been holding on to so tightly for such a long time. Scratch that; she was terrified. But if she never took a chance, she'd never be able to make that dream come true.

That's why she couldn't bring herself to regret falling for Ryan Carter, no matter how painfully things had ended the day before. At least she'd tried…at least she'd opened herself to the possibility that maybe, just maybe, he could have been The One. Sure, she'd crashed and burned. But at least she hadn't vomited on Ryan's feet. She'd lost a piece of her heart to Ryan and his darling little boy—a big piece. She'd never get it back, but even as she'd cried herself to sleep the night before, she hadn't been sorry for risking it all. If she'd had the chance to do it all over again, she would have only changed one decision.

She would have told Ryan she loved him.

It was her one regret. What's the worst thing that could have happened? If he hadn't said it back, it wouldn't have been the end of the world. Loving someone was never a mistake. She'd learned that lesson a long time ago from the shelter animals. Love in its purest form was unconditional.

"I need to choose one of these furry little guys to take out for a walk," Amanda said, glancing from one enclosure to the next. "Do you have any suggestions?"

"I do, actually." Birdie cleared her throat and nodded to a spot over Amanda's shoulder. "How about that one?"

Amanda turned around.

The dog that Birdie was looking at wasn't locked in a kennel. He was standing in the center aisle on short, stubby legs, looking up at Amanda with a furrow in his grumpy little brow. He also had a tiny lace-trimmed pillow secured to his back with something shiny tied to it with a white satin bow.

What was happening?

"Tucker? What are you doing here?" Amanda moved closer so she could scoop the dog into her arms, but as soon as she caught a definite glimpse of the diamond ring attached to the tiny cushion on his back, she froze.

Oh my God.

Then she looked around, because she knew Ryan had to be here somewhere, and he was. He was walking up the center aisle behind Tucker, and Dillon was there too, flashing the same bashful smile that had stolen her heart the first time she'd ever seen him, quietly clutching his plastic dinosaur at the Grille.

"Hi," she said, choking on a sob.

"Don't cry, love." Ryan reached for her, pulling her into his arms and holding her as she gave way to the tears she couldn't hold back any longer. "I'm sorry. So, so sorry. I should have asked you to stay. I *wanted* you to stay. I went to find you at the Grille, but Paul told me you'd come to walk dogs. So here we are, and I'm ready to tell you exactly how I feel. I love you with my whole heart. I was just worried I hadn't changed enough to give you the kind of life you deserve."

"What?" She sniffed as he cupped her face with his hands and wiped away tear after tear with the pads of his thumbs. "But you have changed."

"Because *you* changed me, Amanda. Knowing you has made me a better man, a good man. A good father. And, if you say yes, a good husband too."

Then he dropped down to one knee right there on the shelter's concrete floor—this man she'd so recently lost. He was sorry, and he loved her. But perhaps most important, he'd become her home.

"Yes." She nodded and held out her hand as Dillon

tried to untangle the ring from the pillow on Tucker's back while the dog started chasing his tail.

"Wait! Bunny needs to see this!" Birdie threw her hands in the air and dashed out of the building. "Don't go anywhere. You can do a reenactment."

"Don't worry." Ryan laughed. "I don't think we'll need a reenactment. We might be here a while."

"Stay still, Tucker," Dillon said.

Did the petulant little chiweenie listen? Of course not.

And Amanda wouldn't have had it any other way. *There's no place like home.*

* * * * *

Look for the next book in the
Furever Yours continuity,
Not Just the Girl Next Door
by Stacy Connelly.

On sale March 2019,
wherever Harlequin Special Edition
books and ebooks are sold.

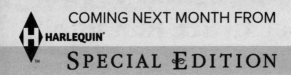
#2677 TEXAN SEEKS FORTUNE
The Fortunes of Texas: The Lost Fortunes • by Marie Ferrarella
Connor Fortunado came to Houston with only one agenda: tracking down a missing Fortune relative. His new assistant, single mom Brianna Childress, is a huge help and their attraction is instant—even though the last thing the bachelor Fortune wants is a houseful of commitments!

#2678 ANYTHING FOR HIS BABY
Crimson, Colorado • by Michelle Major
Paige Harper wants her inn, and Shep Bennett—the developer who bought it out from under her—needs a nanny. But Paige is quickly falling for little Rosie and is finding Shep more and more attractive by the day...

#2679 THE BABY ARRANGEMENT
The Daycare Chronicles • by Tara Taylor Quinn
Divorced after a heartbreaking tragedy, Mallory Harris turns to artificial insemination to have a baby. When her ex-husband learns of her plan, he offers to be the donor. Mallory needs to move on. But how can she say no to the only man she's ever loved?

#2680 THE SEAL'S SECRET DAUGHTER
American Heroes • by Christy Jeffries
When former SEAL Ethan Renault settles in Sugar Falls, Idaho, the last thing he expects to find on his doorstep...is his daughter? He's desperate for help—and librarian Monica Alvarez is just the woman for the job. But Ethan soon realizes his next mission might be to turn their no-strings romance into forever!

#2681 THE RANCHER'S RETURN
Sweet Briar Sweethearts • by Kathy Douglass
Ten years ago, the love of Raven Reynolds's life disappeared without a trace. Now Donovan Cordero is back, standing on her doorstep. Along the way, Raven had the rancher's child—though he didn't know she was pregnant! But how can she rebuild a life with her child's father if she's engaged to another man?

#2682 NOT JUST THE GIRL NEXT DOOR
Furever Yours • by Stacy Connelly
Zeke Harper has always seen Mollie McFadden as his best friend's sister. He can't cross the line, no matter how irresistible he finds the girl next door. Until Mollie makes the first move! Now Zeke wonders if this woman who opens her life to pets in need can find a place for him in her heart.

Get 4 FREE REWARDS!

We'll send you 2 FREE Books plus 2 FREE Mystery Gifts.

Harlequin® Special Edition books feature heroines finding the balance between their work life and personal life on the way to finding true love.

FREE
Value Over
$20

YES! Please send me 2 FREE Harlequin® Special Edition novels and my 2 FREE gifts (gifts are worth about $10 retail). After receiving them, if I don't wish to receive any more books, I can return the shipping statement marked "cancel." If I don't cancel, I will receive 6 brand-new novels every month and be billed just $4.99 per book in the U.S. or $5.74 per book in Canada. That's a savings of at least 12% off the cover price! It's quite a bargain! Shipping and handling is just 50¢ per book in the U.S. and 75¢ per book in Canada.* I understand that accepting the 2 free books and gifts places me under no obligation to buy anything. I can always return a shipment and cancel at any time. The free books and gifts are mine to keep no matter what I decide.

235/335 HDN GMY2

Name (please print)

Address   Apt. #

City   State/Province   Zip/Postal Code

Mail to the Reader Service:
IN U.S.A.: P.O. Box 1341, Buffalo, NY 14240-8531
IN CANADA: P.O. Box 603, Fort Erie, Ontario L2A 5X3

Want to try 2 free books from another series! Call 1-800-873-8635 or visit www.ReaderService.com.

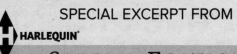
"You'll still get plenty of time with him," Raven said as Elias
ran off.

"You're being nicer about this than I'd expected you to be."

"What did you think I'd do? Grab my kid and go sneaking off
in the middle of the night?"

Donovan inhaled a sharp breath.

"Sorry. I didn't mean that the way it sounded."

"I'm just a bit sensitive, I guess."

"And I'm a bit uncomfortable. Have you noticed how many
people are staring at us?"

"They're not staring at us. They're staring at you. You're the
prettiest girl here."

Raven laughed. "There's no need for flattery. I already said you
can spend time with Elias."

"It's not flattery. It's the truth. You're gorgeous."

The laughter vanished from her voice and the sparkle left her eyes. "No flirting. We're not on a date. We're here for Elias."

"But we are getting to know each other. Not for the purpose of falling in love again. I know you're engaged and I respect that."

"Who told you I was engaged?"

"Carson. Congratulations, I hope you'll be happy together. Just so you know, I have no intention of interfering in your life. But if we're going to coparent Elias, we need to find a way to be friends again. And we were friends, weren't we?"

She nodded and the smile reappeared. Apparently he'd said the right thing.

Donovan stepped in front of Raven and took her hands in his. Though she worked on the ranch, her palms were soft. "I'm sorry."

"Sorry for what?"

"For putting you through ten years of hell. Ten years of hoping I'd come home. For not being around while you were pregnant or to help you raise our son. All of it. I'm sorry for all of it. Please forgive me."

Her eyes widened in surprise and she blinked. Was what he'd said so unexpected? He didn't think so. Just what kind of jerk did she think he'd become? He replayed the conversation they'd had that first night. It must have looked like he was playing games when he hadn't fully answered her questions. But Raven was engaged to another man, so his reasons for staying away really didn't matter now. They'd have to start here to build their relationship.

"You're forgiven."

"Clean slate?"

She smiled. "Clean slate. Now let's catch up to Elias and play some games. I plan on winning one of those oversize teddy bears."

Don't miss
The Rancher's Return *by Kathy Douglass,*
available March 2019 wherever
Harlequin® Special Edition books and ebooks are sold.

www.Harlequin.com

#1 *New York Times* bestselling author

LINDA LAEL MILLER

presents:

**The next great contemporary read from
Harlequin Special Edition author Kathy Douglass!
A heartwarming story about finding community,
friendship and even love.**

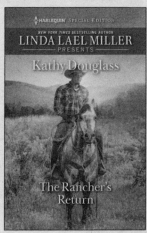

**"That's all you have to
say? You're back now?"**

Ten years ago, the love
of Raven Reynolds's life
disappeared without a trace.
Now Donovan Cordero
is back, standing on her
doorstep. Along the way,
Raven had the rancher's
child—though he didn't
know she was pregnant!
Now her prayers have been
answered, but happily-ever-
after feels further away than
ever. Because how can she rebuild a life with her child's
father if she's engaged to another man?

**Available February 19,
wherever books are sold.**

www.Harlequin.com

HSELLM57364

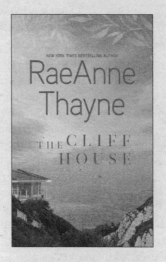

Love Harlequin romance?

DISCOVER.

Be the first to find out about promotions, news and exclusive content!

Facebook.com/HarlequinBooks

Twitter.com/HarlequinBooks

Instagram.com/HarlequinBooks

Pinterest.com/HarlequinBooks

ReaderService.com

EXPLORE.

Sign up for the Harlequin e-newsletter and download a free book from any series at **TryHarlequin.com.**

CONNECT.

Join our Harlequin community to share your thoughts and connect with other romance readers!
Facebook.com/groups/HarlequinConnection

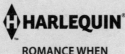

HARLEQUIN®

**ROMANCE WHEN
YOU NEED IT**

HSOCIAL2018

Reward the book lover in you!

Earn points on your purchase of new Harlequin books from participating retailers.

Turn your points into **FREE BOOKS** of your choice!

Join for FREE today at **www.HarlequinMyRewards.com**.

Harlequin My Rewards is a free program (no fees) without any commitments or obligations.